Roy Blakeley's Motor Caravan

Percy Keese Fitzhugh

ROY BLAKELEY'S MOTOR CARAVAN

CHAPTER I – SOME EXPEDITION!

Gee whiz, whenever I see that fellow Harry Domicile, I know there's going to be a lot of fun. Just the same as I can always tell if we're going to have mince turnovers for dessert. That's one thing I'm crazy about—mince turnovers. I can tell when I go through the kitchen if we're going to have them, because our cook has a kind of a look on her face. I can eat five of those things at a sitting, but that isn't saying how many I can eat standing up. Pee-wee Harris can eat seven, even while he's talking at the same time. Anyway, that hasn't got anything to do with Harry Donnelle.

Maybe you're wondering why I named this chapter "Some Expedition." If it was about Pee-wee Harris, I'd name it "Some Exhibition," because that kid is a regular circus. So now I guess I'll tell you.

One afternoon I was sitting on the railing of our porch taking a rest after mowing the lawn. I was thinking how it would be a good idea if they had lawn mowers that run by gas engines. We've got a great big lawn at our house. At Doc Carson's house they have a little bit of a lawn—he's lucky. Gee whiz, you could cut that lawn with a safety razor.

All of a sudden I saw Harry Donnelle coming up the street. I guess maybe you know who he is, because we had some adventures with him in other stories. He's a big fellow, I guess he's about twenty-five. He was a lieutenant in the war. My sister likes him a lot only she said I mustn't say so in a story. I should worry about her. He comes up to our house a lot. Believe me, that fellow's middle name is adventure. He says all his ancestors were crazy about adventures. He says he wouldn't have any ancestors unless they were. He says that's why he picked them out. Gee williger, you ought to hear him jollying Pee-wee. He told Pee-wee that once he lived in obscurity and Pee-wee wanted to know where that was. Can you beat that? Harry told him it was in Oregon. Good night!

So as soon as I saw that fellow coming up across the lawn, I kind of knew there was going to be something doing. Because only a few days before that he had told me that maybe he would want my patrol to help him in a daring exploit. Oh, boy, those are my favorite outdoor sports — daring exploits. I eat them alive.

He said, "Hello, kid, I went fishing with Jake Holden last night and we got into a school of perch."

I said, "Don't talk about school; this is vacation."

He had a bundle with some perch in it and he said they were for supper. So I took them into the kitchen and while I was in there I ate some icing off a cake. If I had my way cakes would be all icing, but our cook says you have to have a foundation to put the icing on. Me for the roof.

When I went back Harry said, "I suppose you kids will be starting for that old dump up in the Catskills pretty soon." He meant Temple Camp. I said, "We take our departure in two weeks."

He said, "Take your which?"

I said, "Our departure; don't you know what that is?"

"Well," he said, kind of puzzled like, "I guess I'll have to pike around and get some assistance somewhere else. I've got a little job on hand that I thought might interest you and your patrol. Ever hear of the Junkum Corporation, automobile dealers? They have the agency for the Kluck car. They're down in New York. It wasn't anything much; just a little hop, skip, and a jump out west, and back again."

"In junk cars — I mean Kluck cars?" I blurted out.

"Mostly junk," he said; "but of course, as long as your plans are made— —"

"Never you mind about our plans," I told him; "tell me all about it." Because, gee, I was all excited.

He said, "Well, there isn't much to it; just a little gypsy and caravan stuff, as you might say. My sister's husband's brother, Mr. Junkum, is tearing his hair out and lying awake nights, because he can't get cars here from the west. He says the customers are standing on line and all that sort of thing and that everything is clogged up at the other end, the railroads are all tied up in a knot, the freight is piled up as high as the Woolworth building and nothing short of a good dose of dynamite will loosen up the freight congestion out west. If it was a matter of Ford cars he could get them through by parcel post, but with these big six cylinder Klucks it's a different proposition. He's got three touring cars and a big motor van waiting for shipment out in Klucksville, Missouri, and if he can't make deliveries in a couple of weeks or so his customers are going to cancel. Poor guy, I'm sorry for him."

That's just the way Harry talks. He said, "One of those cars, the big enclosed van, is for Jolly and Kidder's big store in New York."

"That's where I bought my last scout suit, at Jolly and Kidder's," I told him.

Then he said, "Junkum wanted me to see if I couldn't round up two or three fellows and bang out to Klucksville and bring the cars home under their own power. I told him the roads were punk and he said it's punk to have your business canceled, so there you are."

"Oh, bibbie," I said, "we'd love to do that only we can't run cars on account of not being old enough."

Then he said, "I rounded up Tom Slade and he agreed to die for the cause—said his vacation was at my disposal. He drove a motor truck in France and he's a bug on good turns. Rossie Bent has promised to run one of the touring cars, I'm going to run the van myself and that leaves one touring car. I tried to get Brent Gaylong on the long distance 'phone up at Newburgh to-day, but he wasn't home—out grouching around, I suppose. His mother said she'd have him call me up or wire me. All I want now is a commissary department and I got a kind of a hunch that maybe you kids could camp in the van and cook for the crowd and make yourselves generally useful. The way I figure it out by the road map there'll be long stretches of road where we won't bunk into any towns. I figured on taking Pee-wee along as a kind of a mascot; you know those little fancy jim-cracks they put on radiator caps in autos? I thought he could be one of those, as you might say, and bring us good luck. He'd be a whole commissary department in himself, I suppose, considering the way he eats. But if you can't you can't, and that's all there is about it."

"What do you mean, we can't?" I shouted at him. "You make me tired! Do you suppose Temple Camp is going to run away just because my patrol is a couple of weeks late getting there? You bet your life we'll go. If you try to sneak off without us, we'll come after you. We're coming back in that motor van, so that's settled. I should worry about Temple Camp."

He just sat there on the railing alongside of me, laughing.

He said, "I thought it would hit you."

"Hit me!" I told him. "Believe me, it gave me a knockout blow."

He said he'd stay to supper so as to talk my mother and father into it, because they don't care anything about making long trips in motor vans and things like that, and maybe they'd say I'd better not go.

But, believe me, Harry Domicile knows how to handle mothers and fathers all right, especially mothers. So don't you worry, just leave it to him.

The worst is yet to come.

II—WHO WE ALL ARE

What do you think my father said? He said he wished he was young enough to go along. Oh, but he's a peach of a father! So is my mother. My sister Marjorie said she'd like to go too. Harry said that no girls were allowed. He said that girls were supposed to stay home and receive picture post-cards. Gee whiz, I'm sorry for them. I'm glad I'm not a girl. But if I wasn't a boy I'd like to be a girl.

That night we had our regular troop meeting. Cracky, you can't get that bunch quiet enough to tell them anything. You know how it sounds in a graveyard? And you know how it sounds in a saw mill? Well, a graveyard sounds like a saw mill compared with the noise at one of our meetings. So I told our scoutmaster, Mr. Ellsworth, that I had something to say and he said they should let me have the chair. Then they began throwing chairs at me. It's good he didn't tell them to let me have the floor, or they'd have ripped that up, I suppose.

"I'd like to get your ear," I shouted.

"You'll get our goat if you don't say what you've got to say," Doc Carson yelled.

"I'm trying to say it if I can get your ear," I said.

"You can have anything except my mouth," Pee-wee piped up. Good night, he needs that.

Then Mr. Ellsworth got them all quieted down and I told them how Harry Domicile wanted the Silver Fox Patrol (that's my patrol) to go out west and how he wanted Pee-wee to go too, even though he was one of the raving Ravens. I said the reason he wanted Pee-wee to go was so he could blow up the tires and we wouldn't have to have any pump. Pee-wee likes auto tires, because they're the same shape as doughnuts—that's what I told him.

There's one good thing about our troop and that is that one patrol never gets jealous of another. If my patrol gets a chance to go somewhere the other fellows don't get mad, because they get more to eat. Absence makes

6

the dessert last longer. In our troop each patrol does as it pleases — united we stand, divided we sprawl. Each patrol always has more fun than the other patrols. So if everybody has more fun than anybody else, they ought to be satisfied, I should hope. Pee-wee is in the Ravens, because he got wished onto them when the troop started, but he belongs to all three patrols, kind of. That's because one patrol isn't big enough for him. He spreads out over three.

So this is the last you'll see of the Ravens and the Elks in this story. Maybe you'll say thank goodness for that. They went up to Temple Camp. There were fifty-three troops up there and everybody had more dessert because Pee-wee wasn't there. So that shows you how my patrol did a good turn for Temple Camp. Gee whiz, you have to remember to do good turns If you're a scout.

Now this story is all about that trip that we made to bring back those four machines, and believe me, we had some adventures. If you were to see Jolly and Kidder's big delivery van now, all filled up with bundles and things C. O. D., you'd never suppose it had a dark past. But, believe me, that past was darker than the Dark Ages. You learn about the Dark Ages in the fifth grade — that's Miss Norton's class. She's my favorite teacher because she has to go to a meeting every afternoon and she can't keep us in.

So now I guess I'll start. The next morning who should show up but Brent Gaylong. He didn't even bother to wire. He said he didn't believe in telegrams and things like that when it came to adventures. He's awful funny, that fellow is — kind of sober like. He's head of a troop up in Newburgh and we met him when we were on a hike once. He can drive a Ford so easy that you don't know it's moving. He says most of the time it's not moving. He's crazy about adventures. Good night, when he and Harry Domicile start talking, we have to laugh. He said he'd do anything provided we got into trouble. Harry told him there ought to be plenty of trouble between Missouri and New York. That fellow tries awful hard to get arrested but he never can.

Now I'll tell you about the other fellows. Harry was the captain—he had charge of the whole outfit. I bet Mr. Junkum trusted him a lot. But one thing, Harry never does anything for money. He says money is no good except when it's buried in the ground and you go and try to find it. That's the kind of a fellow he is. He didn't get killed three times in France. But he came mighty near it. He's got the distinguished service cross. He lives in Little Valley near Bridgeboro. Bridgeboro is my town. I don't mean I own it. Harry's got a dandy Cadillac car of his own. He takes my sister Marjorie out in it.

There was one other big fellow that went on that trip and that was Rossie Bent who works in the bank. He got his vacation especially so he could go. He's got light hair. Often when he sees me he treats me to a soda.

Tom Slade went so as to drive the fourth car, and he's a big fellow too, only you bet your life I'll never call him a big fellow, because before he went to the war he was in our troop. And even now he's just like one of us scouts. I guess maybe you know all about him. Believe me, the war changed him more than it changed the map of Europe.

That leaves Pee-wee and the rest of the fellows in my patrol. So now I'll tell you about them. First comes Roy Blakeley (that's me), and I'm patrol leader. That's what makes me look so sober and worried like. I have to take strawberry sundaes to build me up, on account of the strain of managing that bunch. Next comes Westy Martin; he's my special chum. He's got eleven merit badges. He's awful careful. He does his homework as soon as he gets home every day, so in case he gets killed it will be done. I should worry about my homework if I got killed. Next comes Dorry Benton, only he was in Europe with his mother so he didn't go with us. If he had gone with us he would have been there. Hunt Manners couldn't go because his brother was going to be married. The rest of the fellows were Charlie Seabury and Will Dawson and the Warner twins, Brick and Slick. They're just the same, only each one of them is smarter than the other. You can't tell which is which, only one of them likes potatoes and the other doesn't. That's the way I tell them apart. If I see one of them eating potatoes I know it's Slick. That leaves only one fellow, and gee whiz, I'm going to give him a chapter all to himself and I hope he'll be satisfied. Some day he'll have a whole book to himself, I suppose. Good night!

III — WHO IS PEE-WEE HARRIS, AND IF SO, WHY?

Anyway Pee-wee Harris is, that's one sure thing. His mother calls him Walter and my sisters call him Walter, but Pee-wee is his regular name. He's our young hero and some of the fellows call him Peerless Pee-wee, and some of them call him Speck.

If all of us fellows were automobiles, Pee-wee would be a Ford. That's because he's the smallest and he makes the most noise. He eats all his food running on high. He never has to shift his gears to eat dessert. Even if it's a tough steak he takes it on high. He's a human cave. He's about three feet six inches in diameter and his tongue is about six feet three inches long. He has beautiful brown curly hair and he's just too cute—that's what everybody says. His nose has got three freckles on it. He starts on compression. When he gets excited Webster's Dictionary turns green with envy.

Now the way it was fixed was that we were all to meet at the Bridgeboro Station at three o'clock the next day so as to get the three-eighteen train for New York. Then we were going to go on the Lake Shore Limited to Klucksville—that's near St. Louis.

When Pee-wee showed up at the station he looked like the leader of a brass band. His scout suit was all pressed, his compass was dangling around his neck, in case the Lake Shore Limited should lose its way, I suppose, and his scout knife was hanging to his belt. He had his belt-ax on too. I guess that was so he could chop his way through the forests if the train got stalled. He had his camera and his air rifle and his swamp boots and his scout whistle, and he had his duffel bag on the end of his scout staff. And, oh, boy, he had a new watch.

I said, "Good night, you must have been robbing the church steeple. Where did you get that young clock? If it only had an electric bulb in it we could use it for a headlight. Is it supposed to keep time?"

"It ought to be able to keep a whole lot of time, it's big enough," Harry said. "Are you going to take it with you or send it by express?"

I said, "Oh, sure, a big watch like that can keep a lot of time; it holds about a quart."

"You make me tired!" Pee-wee shouted. "It's warranted for a year."

"I bet it takes a year to wind it up," Westy said.

"Anyway we can drink out of it if we get thirsty," Will Dawson told him. "It's got a nice spring in it."

"It doesn't vary a second," Pee-wee shouted. "Look at the clock in the station; that's Western Union time."

Gee whiz, but that kid was proud of his new watch. He looked at it about every ten seconds while we were waiting for the train, and every once in a while he looked up at the sun. I guess maybe he thought the sun was a little late, hey? When we got to the city he checked up all the clocks he saw on the way over to the Grand Central Station, to see if they were right, and when we were whizzing up along the Hudson on the Lake Shore Limited he kept a time table in one hand and his watch in the other so as to find out if we reached Poughkeepsie and Albany on time.

Just before we all turned in for the night, Harry and Brent Gaylong went over and sat by him and began jollying him about the watch. The rest of us sprawled around on the Pullman seats, listening and laughing. Gee whiz, when Harry and Brent Gaylong get together, good night!

Harry said, "The trouble with those heavy duty watches is they're not intended for night work. They work all right in the daytime, but you see at night when they haven't got the sun to go by, they get to sprinting— —"

"Do you know what kind of a watch this is?" Pee-wee shouted at him. "It's a scout watch— —"

Brent said in that sober way of his, "That's just the trouble. Those scout watches go scout-pace. A scout is always ahead of time; so is a scout watch.

If a scout watch is supposed to arrive at three o'clock, it arrives at two — an hour beforehand. A scout is prompt."

"Positively," Harry said; "by to-morrow morning that watch will be an hour ahead of time. It'll beat every other watch by an hour."

"I bet it's right on the minute to-morrow morning," Pee-wee shouted. "That's a scout watch; it's advertised in Boys' Life. The ad. said it keeps perfect time."

"How long have you had it?" Rossie Bent wanted to know.

"My father gave it to me for a present on account of this trip," the kid said; "he gave it to me just before I started off."

"So you haven't had it overnight yet?" Brent asked him. "You don't know whether it's good at night work or not."

"They always race in the dark," Harry said; "that's the trouble with those boy scout watches."

By this time the colored porter and about half a dozen passengers were standing around listening and laughing.

Harry said, "Well, I'll tell you what I'll do, Kid. I happen to know something about those watches and they're not to be trusted. The boy scout watch is a pile of junk. If that watch isn't at least an hour ahead of time when we sit down to breakfast to-morrow morning, I'll buy you the biggest pie they've got in the city of Cleveland. If your watch is wrong by as much as an hour you'll have to do a good turn between every two stations we stop at till we get to Chicago. What do you say?"

"I won't have to worry about any good turns," Pee-wee shot back at him.

Harry said, "All right, is it a go?"

"Sure it's a go," the kid shouted. "Mm! Mm! I'll be eating pie all day to-morrow."

CHAPTER IV — PEE-WEE'S WATCH

I guess Pee-wee dreamed of pie that night. Anyway he didn't wake up very early in the morning. When the train stopped at Cleveland for eats, he was dead to the world. The rest of us all went into the railroad station for breakfast and Harry took a couple of sandwiches and a hard boiled egg and a bottle of milk back to the train for our young hero when he should wake up.

When we were eating breakfast in the station, Harry said, "Well, I see that none of you kids has ever been out west before. Hadn't we better set our watches?"

I looked up at the clock in the station and, good night, then I knew why he and Brent had been jollying Pee-wee the night before. The dock in the station was an hour behind my watch.

"Western time, boys," Harry said; "set your watches back."

"And keep still about it when you go back on the train," Rossie said, "if you want to see some fun."

"We've lost an hour," Westy said.

"Don't you care," Brent said; "don't bother looking for it; we'll find it coming back."

Gee whiz, I had to laugh when I thought of Pee-wee lying sound asleep in his upper berth with his trusty boy scout watch under his pillow. When we went back on the train all the berths except Pee-wee's were made into seats. There were only about a half a dozen passengers besides ourselves in that car, and Harry went around asking them all not to mention to Pee-wee about western time.

I guess it was about a half an hour later the kid woke up. He was so sleepy that he never thought about the time till after he had got washed and dressed, then he came staggering through the car wanting to know where we were. The rest of us were all sprawling in the seats and the passengers were smiling, because I guess they knew what was coming.

Harry said, "Sit down here and have some breakfast, Kid. We thought we wouldn't bother you to get up when we stopped in Cleveland. What time have you got?"

Pee-wee hauled out his old boy scout turnip and said, "It's half past nine."

Harry said, "Oh, not quite as bad as that; boy scouts don't sleep till half past nine. It's just—let's see—it's just about half past eight." Then he showed his watch to Pee-wee, kind of careless like.

By that time we were all crowding around waiting to see the fun and the passengers were all looking around and kind of smiling.

Harry said, "Sit down and eat your breakfast, Kid, and don't let that old piece of junk fool you. What time have you got, Roy?"

I could hardly keep a straight face, but I said, "About half past eight."

"You see, it's just as I told you, Kid," Harry said. "As soon as you go to sleep those boy scout watches take advantage of you. I wouldn't trust one of them any more than I'd trust a pickpocket. How about that, Brent?"

"Oh, I've met some pretty honest pickpockets," Brent said. "Of course, some of them are dishonest. But it's the same as it is in every other business; some are honest and some are not. I've seen some good, honest, hard working pickpockets. What time is it, Tom Slade?"

Gee whiz, I was afraid when Tom took out his watch, because he usually stands up for Pee-wee, and I was afraid he'd let him know. But he just looked at his watch, very sober, and said, "Pretty nearly twenty minutes of nine."

"You all make me sick!" Pee-wee yelled. "You think you're smart, don't you? You all got together and changed your watches."

"This is the same watch I always carried," Brent said.

"I mean you all changed the time," Pee-wee shouted; "you think you can put one over on me, don't you?"

"That watch would be all right for a paperweight, Kid," Rossie said, "or for an anchor when you go fishing."

"It's all right to keep time, too," the kid shouted.

"It doesn't keep it, it lets it out," Harry said; "did you have the cover closed? A whole hour has sneaked away on you."

"Maybe it leaks a little," Brent said.

"There may be a short circuit in the minute hand," Harry said.

"That watch is right!" the kid shouted. "That's a boy scout watch and it's guaranteed for a year."

"Well, it's an hour ahead of the game," Harry said. "You ask any one of these gentlemen the correct time."

Oh, boy, I had to laugh. Pee-wee went through the aisle holding his precious old boy scout watch in his hand, asking the different passengers what time it was. Every single one of them took out his watch and showed the kid how he was an hour wrong. All of a sudden, in came the conductor and Harry winked at him and said, "What's the correct time, Cap?"

"Eight thirty-eight," the conductor said.

Harry said, "There you are, Kiddo; what have you got to say now?"

Gee whiz, the kid didn't have anything to say. He just stood there gaping at his watch and then staring around and the passengers could hardly keep straight faces.

The conductor caught on to the joke and he winked at Harry and said, "Those toy watches aren't expected to keep time."

Harry said, "Oh, no, but he'll have a real watch when he grows up. He's young yet. He can take this one apart and have a lot of fun with the works."

"Somebody set this watch ahead—some of you fellows did!" Pee-wee shouted. "It was right last night. It keeps good time. Somebody played a trick on me! This is a what-do-you-call-it—a conspiracy. You're all in it."

Just then we passed a station and there was a clock in a steeple. Harry said, "You don't claim that clock in the church steeple is in the conspiracy, do you? Look at it. Now what have you got to say?"

Then the conductor put his arm over Pee-wee's shoulder and he said, "Didn't you ever hear of western time, son? The next time you're traveling west you just drop an hour at Cleveland station and you'll find it waiting there for you when you come back."

"Sure," I told him; "did you notice that big box on the platform? That's where they keep them. It's all full of hours."

The kid just stood there, staring. I guess he didn't know what to believe.

"Set your watch back an hour and don't let them fool you," the conductor said, and then he began laughing.

"And remember that western time is different from eastern time," Rossie said.

"Oh, sure, everything is different out west," Harry put in. "I like the western time better."

"Eastern time is good enough for me," Brent said; "I always preferred it."

"And if you should ever happen to be crossing the Pacific Ocean on any of your wild adventures, Kid," Harry said, "don't forget to set your watch back one day when you cross the equator."

"If it's one day I wouldn't have to set it back at all," Pee-wee said. "Three o'clock to-day is the same as three o'clock yesterday."

"It would be better to set it back and be sure," Harry said.

"Oh, yes, safety first," Brent said; "there might be a slight difference. One three o'clock might look like another, but there's a difference."

"How do you know when you cross the equator?" I asked Harry.

He said, "You can tell by the bump. Sometimes the ship just glides over it easily and you can't tell at all unless you look."

"It's best to shift gears going over the equator," Brent said; "go into second and stay in second till you get up the hill."

"What hill?" Pee-wee wanted to know. "You make me sick; there aren't any hills on the ocean."

"That's where you're wrong," Rossie Brent said. "If you go to Coney Island and watch a ship coming toward you from way out on the ocean, you see the top of the masts first, don't you? Then after a while you see the whole ship. That's because it's coming up hill. See?"

"You should worry about hills, Kid," I said; "go ahead and eat your breakfast."

V — THE CARAVAN

I guess by now you must think we're all crazy; I should worry. I just thought I'd tell you that about Pee-wee's watch because, gee, it had us all laughing. So already you've lost an hour reading this story; don't you care.

Now we didn't have any more adventures on that trip. We didn't do much except eat and, gee whiz, you wouldn't call that having adventures. Late that night we got to Klucksville and we stayed at the hotel till morning. They have dandy wheat cakes at that hotel. And syrup, mm, mm! Then we went to the auto works and the four cars were all ready for us, because Mr. Junkum had sent a telegram to say we were coming.

Oh, boy, you should have seen that big van, a regular gypsy wagon. On the outside was painted,

JOLLY & KIDDER

THE MAMMOTH STORE

EVERYTHING FOR THE HOME

It was all enclosed and there was an electric light inside and steps to go up to it and everything. There were kind of lockers inside too; I guess they were for small bundles, hey? The kind that mothers buy and then send back again, because they don't fit.

Gee whiz, there wasn't much to see in Klucksville. We could have brought the whole town home with us in the van if we had wanted to, — all except the auto works. We didn't waste much time there because Harry wanted to get an early start and go as far as we could the first day. But anyway, we stopped long enough in the village to have a man print a big sign on canvas that we tacked on the van. It said,

MISSOURI TO NEW YORK

SHOULD WORRY ABOUT RAILROADS

BOY SCOUTS ON THE JOB!

WE WORK WHILE OTHERS LOAF

BE PREPARED

Besides that we bought three straw mattresses and an oil stove and some canned stuff. We didn't need to buy much except food, because we had a lot of camping stuff along. We got cans of beans and soup and tuna fish and some egg powder and Indian meal, because I can make lots of things with that. Gee whiz, I can't tell you all the stuff we bought, but if you watch us you'll see us eating it. Believe me, we ate everything except the straw mattresses. Harry said the Kluck was a pretty good car for eating up the miles, but believe me, it hasn't got anything on us when it comes to eating.

Now this is the way we started. First was a touring car with Tom Slade driving it. He's awful sober, kind of. But you can have a lot of fun with him. He has no use for candy, but he's got a lot of sense about other things. I can always make him laugh—leave it to me. Next came another touring car with Rossie Bent driving it. He had a pasteboard sign on his and it said,

WE'RE FROM MISSOURI,

WE'LL SHOW YOU

Next came Brent Gaylong in the other touring car and he had a pasteboard sign that said,

YOU'RE IN LUCK

IF YOU GET A KLUCK

FROM THE WOOLLY WEST

BOUND FOR LITTLE OLD NEW YORK;

After that came the big van with Harry driving it.

Now we fellows were supposed to live in the van, but we didn't do much except sleep in it. Most of the time we were riding in the different cars. A lot of the time I sat with Tom Slade. Mostly the Warner twins rode in the car with Rossie Bent. Charlie Seabury and Westy were in Brent Gaylong's car a lot of the time. Will Dawson got sleepy a lot so he was in the van mostly. Pee-wee rode in all the different cars at once, but most of the time in the van, on account of that being the commissary department. Wherever you see a commissary department, look for Pee-wee. Commissary is his middle name. Sometimes he was up on top of the van dancing around. He's awful light on his feet. He came near lighting on his head a couple of times.

So now I'm going to tell you about that trip.

VI—STRANDED

I guess you'll say this story is a lot of nonsense, but anyway, those big fellows were worse than the rest of us. Harry said it didn't make any difference if we were foolish, because even a dollar hasn't as much cents as it used to have — that's a joke. Anyway Harry had plenty of dollars that Mr. Junkum gave him for expenses. He told us the people who were buying the cars paid part of the money. And anyway, my patrol saved them some money on account of knowing all about camping and cooking and all that. Harry said it was more fun than if we stayed at hotels all the time. Gee whiz, I hate hotels — hotels and spinach. But once I went to a peach of a fire when a hotel burned down. That's one good thing about hotels, anyway.

Now about noontime that day the road crossed the railroad station at a place called Squash Centre. It crosses it there every day, I guess, Sundays and holidays and all. Anyway, it crossed it there that day. Pee-wee was sitting on the seat beside Harry and he shouted, "Squash Centre; I like pumpkin better." As soon as he saw the word squash right away he thought about pie.

There were only about six houses there and the railroad station. On the platform were a lot of funny looking people and they had a couple of big dogs tied by ropes. They had a lot of boxes and bags and things standing around them on the platform. Most of the squashes of Squash Centre were standing around a little way off laughing at them. The man that was holding the dogs had on a long black coat and a high hat and he needed to be shaved. His coat didn't have any cloth on the buttons. He had long hair sticking out from under his hat.

Harry said, "Well, well, we sure are out west. Here's poor old Uncle Tom's Cabin, bag and baggage." Then he called down to the man with the black coat and said, "How about you, old top? Stranded?"

Then all the squashes of Squash Centre set up a howl.

The man said, very dignified like, "Thank you, for your inquiry, young sir, and might I ask if you came through Jones' Junction? Are there any trains running?"

By that time our whole caravan had stopped and all the squashes got around and began staring at us.

Harry said, "I don't believe there are any trains except eastern trains. I don't believe there's anything that stops this side of Indianapolis. How far are you going? What's the matter, didn't you hit it right among the squashes?"

The man said, "The squashes are without art or patriotism. I thank you for your information, sir. We are both stalled and stranded. We have neither a train to travel on nor money to travel on it if we had. Our friends have not welcomed us as we hoped they would. We have a promising engagement at Grumpy's Cross-roads some hundred miles distant, where we are under contract with Major Hezekiah Grumpy to give six performances at the Grand Army reunion there. Major Grumpy, sir, fought bravely to stamp out the evil which our play depicts with such pathos." That was just the way he talked.

Harry said, "So they are having a reunion at Grumpy's Cross-roads, are they?"

"A very magnificent affair, sir," that's just what the man said, "and the major has contracted with us for the presentation of our heart stirring drama with the view of having the dramatic part of the celebration appropriate."

Geewhiz, it was awful funny to hear him talk.

VII – A GOOD TURN

That man's name was Archibald Abbington, and he talked dandy, just as if he had learned it out of a book. One of those other people told us that his right name was Henry Flynn. I felt sorry for them, that's one sure thing. And, oh, boy, but those were two peachy dogs they had. The thing those dogs did mostly was to chase Eliza. Miss Le Farge, she was the one that played Eliza. They never let anybody feed the dogs except her, so they'd be sure to chase her.

Harry said, "Why don't you let them chase some of these squashes away? They stand around gaping just as if they never saw a human being before. How far is Grumpy's Cross-roads anyway?"

Mr. Abbington said, "It's a matter of a hundred miles or thereabout." Gee, he was crazy about that word thereabout. Then he said that they had a contract with Major Grumpy to give their first performance the next afternoon at the Grand Army reunion, but he didn't know what they would do because they were stranded.

Harry was awful nice to him. He said, "Well, it looks as if you were in a kind of a tight place, Archy, and I wish we could help you out. We're reproducing the good old times, too, as you might say, with our overland caravan. These are boy scouts who are taking care of our commissary department and this is their gallant leader, Roy Blakeley. How about it, Roy? Do you think we could squeeze in a good turn, just to vary the monotony? You're the boss of that end of the outfit. It would mean driving all night instead of stopping to camp as we meant to do. Let's look on the map and see where Grumpy's Cross-roads is, anyway."

I said, "The more the merrier; I don't care where it is or how long it takes us to get there. We'll take you. That's our middle name, doing good turns."

"We give shows ourselves sometimes," Pee-wee said. "We have a movie apparatus and we give movie shows. But one thing, we've never been stranded."

Brent said in that funny way of his, "But we hope to be, sometime; we can't expect to have everything at once."

Mr. Abbington said, awful dignified like, "We have been stranded many times, sir. I can assure you it is not pleasant, especially when one of our company is ill."

Gee whiz, I could see plain enough that one of them wasn't feeling good; that was the one they called Miss De Voil—she played Topsy. Maybe the squashes disagreed with her, hey?

Harry said, "Well, it's up to you kids, Roy. Grumpy's Cross-roads is east, so it isn't exactly out of our way, only we'll have to hit into a pretty punk road and there'll be no sleeping around the camp-fire to-night. What do you say?"

Mr. Abbington and all the rest of those people looked at us kids awful anxious, sort of. Gee, it made me feel sorry for them. All of a sudden Pee-wee piped up. He said, "Camp-fires aren't the principal things in scouting; good turns come first. Anyway, once I heard that actors always help each other and maybe, kind of, you might say we're actors, because sometimes we give shows."

Mr. Abbington said, "I am delighted to hear that, my young friend. Let me ask you what you have played."

"He plays the harmonica when nobody stops him," Westy said.

I said, "Oh, sure, he's a peachy actor; he plays dominoes and tennis and tiddle-de-winks. The most stirring part he ever plays is when he stirs his coffee."

Miss Le Farge said to another one of those ladies, "Oh, isn't he just too cute?"

So then we helped them get all their stuff into the van. They had a tent and a lot of other things. Harry whispered to me that he guessed they hadn't had any supper and he said he was afraid if we didn't give them something to eat the man that played the slave driver wouldn't have strength enough to whip Uncle Tom the next afternoon. Brent said maybe even Uncle Tom wouldn't have strength enough to stand up and be whipped. He said, "We'd better feed them up."

So we made a fire in the grove right alongside the road so as not to interfere with Miss De Voil, who was lying on one of the mattresses in the van. We told the ladies that they could have the van all to themselves that night so they could get good and rested. I fried some bacon for them and heated some beans and we got water out of the railroad station.

Gee whiz, the water was the only thing about that railroad that was running.

VIII — GRUMPY

We ran the cars all that night so as to get those people to Grumpy's Cross-roads in the morning. The ladies slept in the van, all except one; she was the one that played Aunt Ophelia. In the play she had to be strict, like a school teacher kind of, with Topsy. But when she wasn't in the play she was awful nice. She sat up all night in Rossie Bent's car, because she said she liked the fresh air. Mr. Abbington and Harry sat together outside the van. I didn't get sleepy much. The rest of the fellows sprawled in Tom Slade's car and Brent Gaylong's car, and were dead to the world. It was nice traveling in the night only we had to go slow. We went across a kind of a prairie and every once in a while we came to farms. It was dandy to see the sun come up in the morning.

About five o'clock we came to a village and we asked a man how far it was to Grumpy's Crossroads. He must have got up before breakfast, that man. He said it was about thirty-five miles, but that we'd have to go very slow on account of the road being all stones. We had to drive those cars easy, because they were supposed to be delivered new.

The man said, "If you're bound east why didn't you hit the south road and cut out Grumpy's Crossroads altogether?"

Harry said, "Because these people have to appear at the Grand Army reunion at Grumpy's Cross-roads this afternoon and we've got to get them there."

The man said, "If that's all you're going to the Cross-roads for, you might as well take the south road. Bill Thorpe, he was t'the Cross-roads yesterday en' he said th' Uncle Tom's Cabin show was called off on 'count of thar bein' no trains runnin'. He said ole Major Grumpy was tearin' 'is hair like a wild Injun at th' railroad unions."

Harry said, "Is that so? Well, I hope he won't have his hair all pulled out by 2 P. M. Do you suppose old Grump ever heard of the Boy Scouts of America?"

"I'll tell him all about them!" Pee-wee shouted. "You just leave it to me."

The man was smoking a pipe and it kind of smelled like a forest fire. It smelled like a forest fire and a gas engine put together, kind of. He laid his pipe down on the step of the van so we'd know that what he was going to say was very serious.

He said, "You take my advice en' daon't mention no scaout boys t'the major; it's like wavin' a red flag before a bull as yer might say."

"Doesn't like 'em, hey?" Harry said.

"Hates 'em," the man said.

"Eats 'em alive, I suppose," Brent said.

"He'd eat 'em raw, only he ain't got teeth enough," the man said.

Brent said in that funny way he has, "Well, I guess that settles it, we'll hit the trail for the Cross-roads; I kind of like old Grump already. I have a kind of a hunch he'll put some pep into this Lewis & Clarke expedition. All we needed to make our joy complete was somebody to try to foil us."

"Cracky, I hope he tries to foil us," Pee-wee piped up.

"Is he a villain?" Brent wanted to know.

"Wall, he ain't just exactly what you might call a villain," the man said, very serious.

Brent said, "Oh, that's too bad. We haven't got a villain for our story yet. I suppose we'll have to advertise when we hit into Indianapolis. 'Wanted, willing and industrious villain; one with some experience preferred; good chance for advancement; duties, being foiled by the Boy Scouts of America.'"

The man said, "Guess you're a kind of a comic, hey?"

"What's the trouble between old Grump and the kids, anyway?" Harry asked him.

The man said, "Wall, naow, I'll tell you. Th' major's an old Civil War man en' he's a great stickler on military training for boys; ain't got no use for studyin' natur' en' all that kind o' thing. He's daft abaout the Civil War, en' he's jest abaout th' biggest old grouch this side o' th' Missippi River. This here reunion o' his, every three years, is the pet uv his heart, as th' feller says. He has th' poor ole veterans limpin' in from miles araound fillin' 'em up with rations en' givin' 'em shows. He's got money enough so's ter make the United States Treasury look like a poor relation; and stingy!"

"That sounds fine," Brent said; "we'll have him eating out of our hands; we'll have him so he comes when we call him. First I was in hopes we might fall in with some train robbers — —"

"Gee, it isn't too late yet!" Pee-wee shouted.

"But a ferocious old major is good enough," Brent said; "we can't expect to have everything. You're positive about his hating the Boy Scouts, are you?" he asked the man. "Because we shouldn't want to count on that and then be disappointed. It's pretty hard when you think you've found a regular scoundrel and then find that you're deceived. Are you willing to guarantee him?"

"Wall, I wouldn' say exactly as he's a villain," the man said; "but he's a ole wild beast, so everybuddy says, en' I'm tellin' yer not to wave no red flag in front uv him with a lot uv this scaout boy nonsense. 'Cause he ain't in the humor, see?"

Harry said, "Do you know, Brent, I think the old codger will do first rate."

"Oh, he'll do," Brent said; "of course, it isn't like finding a pirate, or a counterfeiter, or an outlaw — —"

"You make me tired!" Pee-wee yelled. "If Roy's going to write all this stuff up, we have to have an old grouch, so as we can convert him sort of, don't we, and then he'll — then he'll — what-d'ye-call-it — he'll donate a lot of money and say the boy scouts are all right. I'll manage him, you leave him to me."

Brent said, "You don't happen to know if he has a gold-haired daughter, do you?"

Gee whiz, I guess that man thought we were crazy—I should worry. Even the Uncle Tom's Cabin people were laughing.

Brent said, "Because if our young hero could only rescue old Grump's gold-haired daughter from kidnappers, perhaps old Grump would come across with a real watch that keeps time as a reward for our young hero's bravery. I think we'll have to try our hand with old Grump."

"Are you—are you sure he's mad at the scouts?" Pee-wee wanted to know.

"Tell us the worst," Harry said.

CHAPTER IX — MILITARY PLANS

The man put one foot up on the step of the van and said, "Wall, yer see he owns the Fair Grounds. Thar was a crew uv these here scout kids camping over in the grove to one side of it, and not doin' no manner of harm, I reckon."

"That's one good thing about us, we never do any harm," Pee-wee piped up.

"Wherever they camp the violets spring up," Rossie said.

"Sure, and dandelions and four-leaf clovers, too," the kid shouted.

The man said, "Wall, naow, them kids wasn' doin' no manner uv harm, just cookin' and eatin' — —"

"Gee whiz, they have to do that!" Pee-wee told him. "That's one thing about scouts, they always eat."

"Most always," Harry said.

"En' nothin' would do but he must chase 'em off," the man said. "Some uv them men who wuz interested in the kids made a rumpus about it, but it weren't no good; old Grump said off they must go, and off they went. I wuz sorry ter see it too, hanged if I weren't, because they're a bright, clever lot, them youngsters. Oft times when I'd go inter th' Cross-roads with my old mare marketin', there they'd be in th' grove right alongside th' road, sprawlin' about and onct, when I come away abaout five o'clock in the mornin', thar they were en' give my old mare a drink out uv th' spring."

"Up early, hey?" Harry said.

"Naow, haow is them kids goin' ter hinder th' reunion? That's what I say. Poked away off in th' grove right on ter th' end of the grounds. But the ole major, he says they was nuthin' but a lot uv loafers; wanted to know what good they ever done. Why, Lor' bless me, if he'd a made friends with 'em they might uv helped in the reunion, mightn't they?... Wall, I guess he wuz all piffed abaout the show not bein' able to get there. Trams east of th'

Cross-roads is runnin' all right, but out this way thar ain't been a wheel movin' in a week, 'cept express trains from the east. If I was you fellers I wouldn' go a couple of dozen miles out of my way over a pile of rocks what they call by the name of a road, I wouldn', jus ter do a favor for an old grizzly bear, I wouldn'. Not me."

Gee whiz, Mr. Abbington looked kind of anxious, because Harry just sat there on the seat whistling to himself as if he were thinking. The rest of us were all standing around.

Brent said, "Well, as long as old Grump is a stickler on military training, what do you say we take Grumpy's Cross-roads right under his very nose? We'll make our approach from the west, with our dry-goods delivery van and three five-passenger touring cars. General Harris will have charge of the Commissary. First, the signal corps will communicate with the boy scouts of Grumpy's Cross-roads and advise them that reenforcements are on the way—in a dry-goods van and three touring cars. The grove on the edge of the parade grounds will be in our hands before night. We'll have the Civil War veterans down on their knees begging for an armistice."

"Yes, and maybe—maybe—old Major Grumpy will have to go and live in a castle in Holland, hey?" Pee-wee yelled.

Honest, isn't that kid a scream?

X — THE SIGNAL CORPS AT WORK

First, Harry asked if the telegraph office was open, but it wasn't open. The reason was, because there wasn't any there. If that place had been a little smaller we might have run over it without seeing it and punctured one of our tires.

Then Brent said, "Well then, you don't happen to have a nice hill handy, do you? We'll return it in good condition when we get through with it."

They didn't happen to have any hills in that village — they were out of most everything. Brent said he guessed hills were hard to get. So we started off again and hit into the road that went to Grumpy's Cross-roads. Gee whiz, if Major Grumpy's temper was anything like that road, good night! That was what we all said. But we should worry about the road as long as we had all our plans made. Harry said the Kluck car could eat up the miles all right, but, oh, Sister Anne, if one of them tried eating the miles on that road it would have indigestion, all right. Even Pee-wee couldn't have eaten those.

After we had gone maybe about nine or ten miles we came to a dandy; it was a kind of a young mountain. Now, on the way along, we had been making up a message that we would send by smudge signal, because we thought that if those other scouts got it, it would be a feather in their cap and we were thinking about them more than we were about ourselves. Because a scout is brother to every other scout, see?

So this is the smudge signal that we decided to send, and, good night, little we knew what it would lead to. Pretty soon you'll see the plot beginning to get thicker.

Uncle Tom show will be given as announced.

Deny rumors to contrary.

Boy Scouts of America.

Brent said, "If those kids are up as early as old what's-his-name said they were, they ought to see a smudge signal up on the top of a hill like this, and they can notify old Grump. Then later we'll give him the knockout blow. He'll look like a pancake when we get through with him."

That started Pee-wee off—the word pancake. "We'll go riding into the village, and we'll kind of have our clothes torn, and we'll look all what-d'ye-call-it—weary and footsore—and we'll have all the Uncle Tom's Cabin company sitting in the touring cars," he said, "and we'll have a big sign that says Boy Scouts on the Job, hey? And maybe we'll give a parade."

Harry said, "Well, the best thing for us to do now is to parade up this hill and send the message. You see, although assaults are usually made unknown to the enemy, in this case we'll make a big hit if we start some propaganda along ahead of us. It pays to advertise, as Jolly & Kidder would say."

Now it was a pretty steep climb up to the top of that hill, all woods and jungle. We left the cars down on the road and most of the actor people stayed in them, because they were tired and sleepy. Westy stayed down there so as to cook them some breakfast.

For quite a long distance up that hill we went through thick woods, then we came out into an open place where we could look down and see the road. The autos looked small down there. We could see a little thin line of smoke going up where Westy was starting a fire. The sun was getting brighter and it made Jolly & Kidder's van look all shiny on account of the bright paint on it. It seemed funny to see a department store car away out there in that lonesome country.

Pretty soon we got into more woods and Harry said he guessed there must be a trail. But we couldn't find any.

He said, "This is a forsaken wilderness up here."

"I bet the foot of white man never trod it," Pee-wee said; "I bet it's unknown to civilization up here."

"Well, I guess we're not likely to bunk into any movie shows," Brent said.

Jiminetty, but it was some wild place, all right. We had to go single file and tear away the brush so that we could get through. Tom Slade went ahead, because he can find a trail if there is one, and even if there isn't he always knows how to go. The farther up we went, the worse it got. We couldn't see the road at all on account of the thick woods below us. Gee, it was so still up there that it was sort of spooky.

"I guess no white man ever trod this solemn wilderness before, as our young friend Scout Harris observed," Harry said; "it gets worser and worser."

Just then Tom Slade stopped and we all stopped in his path. In about a jiffy he was down on the ground. Gee whiz, I knew what that meant, for I knew Tom Slade.

"It's a footprint," he said.

Just then we heard a sound right near us, just like branches crackling, and in a couple of seconds one of those bloodhounds from the Uncle Tom's Cabin show came dashing up through the bushes. He pushed Tom Slade right out of the way and began sniffing that footprint. He was so excited that he didn't notice us.

XI – A MYSTERIOUS FOOTPRINT

First it seemed kind of as if that bloodhound was just scooping; that means using something that another scout has found. If I should find a robin's nest and then another scout should stalk there, that would be scooping. Gee whiz, that's a mean thing to do. Up at Temple Camp a scout will get himself disliked for doing that. But it's all right to stalk the cooking-shack. Pee-wee thinks he's the only one who has a right to hang out there – I should worry.

Anyway that has nothing to do with the bloodhound. Tom got out of his way, and we all stood about while the dog sniffed around the footprint, awful excited like. There wasn't another footprint anywhere in sight.

Brent said in that funny way of his, "Well, I guess we're up against the real thing at last. I guess old Snoozer here is on the track of Eliza. Listen and maybe we'll hear her baby crying. She always carries a baby with her when she puts one over on the bloodhounds, doesn't she?"

"You're crazy!" Pee-wee shouted; "she always crosses the ice. Didn't you see that big roll of canvas they've got? That's got ice painted on it. They spread that on the stage and she runs across it with har – what-d'ye-call-it – her infant child."

"Her which?" Harry said.

"I think she takes a thermos bottle, too, and an aluminum cooking set," Brent said.

Harry said, "Well, anyway, she has given old Snoozer the slip this time."

"That's a man's footprint," Pee-wee said; "there's a mystery up here."

"Let's see it," Rossie Bent said; "where is it?"

"You make me sick!" the kid shouted. "How can you see a mystery?"

"You smell it, according to Snoozer," Harry said; "this dog will have a fit in a minute."

35

By that time the dog was pushing every which way in among the bushes and every few seconds coming back to the footprint.

"He seems to be kind of rattled." That's what Harry said.

Pretty soon the dog went running through the bushes out into a big open space that was just about on the top of the mountain. We found out afterward that that was why the mountain was named Bald Head. Gee whiz, he seemed rattled. He'd stop for a couple of seconds and look all around, then start off all of a sudden, then stop again.

Brent said, "Eliza's got his goat this time. Look at old Tomasso there; he's mad because Snoozer took his job."

I looked at Tom Slade (because that's whom he meant) and I saw that he was kind of picking among the bushes over to one side of the big open space. So I went over to where he was and I said, "Tom, what do you think about it? I always thought a bloodhound could follow any trail. That's a fresh footprint too, isn't it? But maybe that dog isn't a real bloodhound, hey?"

Tom said, "He's a real bloodhound, all right, but I don't think he'll find anything."

I said, "Well, how about that footprint then? It was a fresh one. He ought to be able to follow that scent. Gee whiz, I never saw a dog act so funny. He's all rattled and he doesn't know which way to go."

Tom didn't say anything, only he looked over to the open space where the rest of the fellows were watching the dog. By that time the dog was running around and barking, half crazy.

"Eliza fell through the ice," Brent called over to us.

Harry shouted, "She was very poor, she didn't even have a scent. Snoozer's going to have a nervous collapse in a minute; he'll require first aid."

I said to Tom, "Well, somebody was up here, that's sure. That's a new footprint we found. It's plaguey funny that a bloodhound can't follow that trail; I always thought a bloodhound — — "

"A bloodhound isn't a scout," Tom said, kind of sober like, in that way he has; "he followed the trail as far as he could, I suppose. Look around here; don't you see anything?"

That's the way it has always been with Tom Slade ever since he got back from the war. In scouting, he would never do anything himself, but just give us fellows a hint that would start us off. "If you make as good use of your eyes as he makes of his nose, you ought to be able to discover something." That's what he said.

So then I looked all around, and sure enough I could see that the bushes were broken up toward the top and, good night, on one of them was hanging a little piece of rag.

"Some one has been through here," I said, all excited; "why doesn't the dog come over here? The trail leads over this way."

Then I began whistling for the dog and calling to the fellows that we had the trail, and they all started over except the dog. He wouldn't follow them or pay any attention to their whistling and calling, only stayed right where he was running around as if he had a fit.

Before the fellows reached the place where we were Tom said kind of low, "Don't fly off the handle, kid; there are some bushes broken here and a rag. Now what does that mean?"

"It means the trail runs through here," I said; "and that crazy fool of an Uncle Tom's Cabin dog can't follow the scent across that bare place. He's just an actor, that's all that bloodhound is. All he's good for is chasing Eliza."

Tom just took the rag from me and looked at it. "Well then, if the trail runs through here, where are the footprints?" he asked me.

"And the dog doesn't seem to think it's worth bothering about," he said.

"You admit somebody went through here?" I shouted at him.

"Oh, somebody went through here, all right," he said.

"And didn't leave any footprints and didn't leave any scent," I came back at him.

"Only a rag," he said.

By that time the fellows had reached the place where we were. "What's the big idea?" Harry said. "What have you got there?"

Brent said, "As I live, it's a piece of Eliza's dress. The plot grows thicker."

"There isn't a footprint here," I told them.

"She must have slid on the ice," Brent said.

"I'm going to drag that dog over here by the collar," Rossie spoke up.

"It's a mystery," Pee-wee shouted; "it's a deep, dark mystery. We've got to solve it—I mean penetrate it."

Gee whiz, that kid was more excited than the dog.

XII — A DISCOVERY

We all just stood there not knowing what to think. I could tell that Tom Slade had some kind of an idea, but you never catch that fellow shouting out about anything till he's sure. Even when he was a tenderfoot in the troop he was that way.

It seemed mighty funny that we should find just one footprint in those bushes, but maybe there weren't any more across that open space because it was hard and rocky. Anyway, the scent led out into that open space, that was sure. Then on the opposite side of the open space the bushes were broken and there was a rag hanging to one of them. Yet we couldn't get that dog to go all the way across and take up the scent where we found the rag. That was the funny thing. It was funny that there weren't any footprints under those bushes where the rag was hanging, too. Believe me, Pee-wee was right, it was a mystery.

Pretty soon the dog began following the scent back and Will Dawson went after him. In about ten minutes he came up again and said that the dog had followed it as far as a brook where there was a willow tree. He said the dog got rattled there just the same as he did on the summit. So he studied the place carefully and saw that there was a branch of the tree that stuck out over the water and he swung himself across and then back again by that. So he decided that was probably what the man had done on his way up the mountain. So you see that trail was cut in two places.

Will said that he left the dog poking around at the edge of the stream. And that was the last we saw of the dog till we got back to our caravan. Then we saw that he was under the van asleep. He was resting up so he could chase Eliza in the afternoon, that's what Brent said. He chased Eliza twice every day, that bloodhound did.

Harry said, "Well, as Scout Harris says, it's a mystery. Somebody was up here before us, that's sure. There's no use trying to dope it out, I suppose. Let's send the signal. Our friends down below will think we're lost."

All the while Tom Slade was sort of wandering around that rocky open space on the top of the mountain. A couple of times he looked over to where we were as if he was kind of thinking. Most of the time he looked at the ground and the flat rocks. I knew he had some idea in his head, all right.

Pretty soon he came strolling over and said sort of offhand like, "Let's follow these broken bushes in a ways."

"Nobody went through here, Tom," Rossie said; "if they had there'd be footprints. Let's get busy with the smudge signal."

"It'll only take a minute," Tom said.

"Every minute is precious, Tommy boy," Harry told him.

"Sure, let's go in," Brent said; "I'm for adventure every time. You never can tell; come ahead."

So we all followed Tom in. The brush was awful thick and I kept tearing it apart down near the ground, hunting for footprints, but I couldn't find a single one. The brush wasn't even broken above, either, after we had gone a few feet and Tom just pushed around without any signs to go by, all the while squinting his eyes into the bushes and poking the underbrush with his feet.

Pretty soon, good night, Pee-wee gave a shout. "I see it! I see it!" he yelled. "The mystery is solved! I know why there isn't any man's footprint here. It was an animal that came through! There he is now — it's a zebra!"

"A which?" Harry said.

"It's got stripes — wide stripes," the kid shouted. "Look there! See it? It's a zebra! Don't you know a zebra?"

Brent said, "I wouldn't know one if I met him in the street."

By that time Tom had gone ahead of us and hauled something out of the bushes. It wasn't a zebra, but it had stripes all right — it was light colored and it had wide, dark stripes. I bet you can't guess what it was, either.

It was a suit of convicts' clothes.

CHAPTER XIII — TOM SLADE, SCOUT

"Didn't I tell you it had stripes?" Pee-wee shouted. "Wasn't I right? Now you see! A scout is observant."

"If he sees a suit of clothes he thinks it's a zebra," Charlie Seabury said.

Harry said, "Well, you weren't so far wrong, Kiddo. The stripes weren't on an animal; they were on a jail bird. I'd like to know where he flew away to. This is getting interesting. I knew that clothing was very high, but I didn't think we'd find a suit as far up as this."

"Maybe he was a murderer, hey?" Pee-wee whispered.

"We can only hope," Brent said in that funny way. Then he said, "I've always felt that I'd like to be a murderer. I thought I was a real convict when I was held in jail three hours after speeding in my flivver. But when I look at this striped suit, I realize that after all I didn't amount to much as a criminal. Let's take a squint at those clothes, will you? It's always been the dream of my young life to escape from jail by using a hair-pin or a manicure file or some kind of acid. I wonder how this fellow escaped."

"I bet he escaped in the dead of night," Pee-wee said.

"The question is, where is he?" Harry said.

"He went away in an airplane," Tom Slade said, awful sober like, just as if Brent hadn't been joking at all.

Good night, we all just stood there stark still, looking at him.

"What makes you think that?" Rossie wanted to know.

"No one laid that suit of clothes here," Tom said; "it was dropped here. There aren't any footprints. Out there in the flat part there are wheel marks from an airplane. I saw enough of those marks in France to know what they mean."

"Tomasso Nobody Holmes, the boy detective!" I shouted.

"The airplane grazed the bushes when it went up," he said; "that's why some twigs are broken off. And part of one of the wings of the machine was torn, too. That's because the airman didn't have space enough to get away in. He took a big chance when he landed up here, that fellow."

Harry just stood there drumming his fingers on one of the bushes and looking all around him and kind of thinking. Then he said, "What's your idea, Tommy boy? Do you think a convict escaped and made his way up to the top of this jungle and that the airman alighted here for him by appointment?"

"The dog followed the scent out into the open, to the place where the wheel tracks are," Tom said. "That's where the man—that convict—got in. They didn't have open space enough to start from there and they grazed the bushes. I guess it was pretty risky, the whole business. Anyway, they chucked the convict clothes out. This piece of silk is waxed; it's part of the wing of a machine, all right."

"Tomasso, you're a wonder," Rossie said; "no dog could follow a trail in the air."

"There's often a scent in the breeze," Brent said.

"Didn't I tell you it was a mystery?" Pee-wee shouted. "Didn't I tell you it was a dark plot? As soon as I saw those clothes — —"

"You thought they were a zebra," Ralph Warner said; "a scout knows all the different kinds of animals."

"You make me sick!" the kid shouted. "A convict is better than a zebra, isn't he?"

"That's a fine argument," I told him.

"It's logic," the kid shouted.

"Well, let's not complain," Brent said; "a zebra would be a novelty, but a convict is not to be despised. We should be thankful for the convict, even though he isn't here."

"That's the best part of it," the kid shouted; "that makes the mystery. We've got to find him."

We didn't bother any more about the mystery then, because we wanted to send the signal and get started again, but you'll see how that mystery popped up again and confounded us; I guess you know what confounded means, all right. It means the same as baffled, only I didn't know whether baffled has two f's in it or not. But, gee whiz, I used it anyway — I should worry.

So now while our friends are waiting for us down on the road (I got this sentence from Pee-wee), I'll tell you about sending that signal. Signals are my middle name — signals and geography. But the thing I like best about school is lunch hour. I'm crazy about boating, too.

XIV — PEE-WEE'S GOAT

That fellow, Harry Domicile, he's crazy. He said, "If you like signals so much I don't see why you send them. Why don't you keep them?"

Will Dawson said, "It isn't the signal we send, it's a message; we send a message by a signal. See?"

Harry said, "But if it's a good message why should you want to send it away? Why don't you keep it? If it's worth anything what's the use of getting rid of it? A scout should not be wasteful." Then he winked at Brent Gaylong.

Oh, boy, you should have seen Pee-wee. He shouted, "You're crazy! Suppose I keep some-thing — suppose I keep — —"

Rossie said, "Suppose you keep silence."

"That shows how much you know about logic!" the kid yelled. "How can I keep silence — —"

By that time we were all laughing, except Harry. He had the paper with the message written on it and he said, very sober like, "Well, if this message is any good at all I don't see why we don't keep it; it might come in useful."

Pee-wee shouted, "A message is no good at all — even the most important message in the world is no good to the fellow that makes it — —"

Brent said, "Then he's just wasting his time making it. Before we send this message we'd better talk it over. If it's any good we'll keep it."

Gee whiz, you should have seen our young hero; I thought he'd jump off the mountain. He yelled, "Do you know what logic is? You get that in the third grade. My uncle knows a man that's a lawyer and he says — besides — anyway, do you mean to tell me — —"

Harry said, "Go on."

Brent said, "Proceed; we follow you."

"Suppose I had a piece of pie," the kid yelled. "If it was good I'd eat it, wouldn't I?"

Brent said, "That isn't logic."

"Sure it's logic!" Pee-wee shouted. "The better it is the more I'd get rid of, wouldn't I?"

"Thou never spakest a truer word," I told him.

"And it's the same with messages," he said.

I said, "Good night, you don't want to eat it, do you?"

Harry said, "Well, if he doesn't want to eat it, what's the use of chewing it over? Let's send it."

I bet you think we're all crazy, hey? I should worry.

So then we gathered a lot of twigs and started a fire about in the middle of that open space. While we were doing that, Charlie Seabury and Ralph Warner got some dead grass and brush and took it down to the brook and got it good and wet. Then they squeezed the water all out of it so it was kind of damp and muggy like. It has to be just like that if you want to send a smudge message. Maybe you don't know exactly what a smudge signal is because maybe you think that a smudge is just a dirt streak on your face — I don't mean on yours but on Pee-wee's. That's Pee-wee's trade mark — a smudge on his face. Usually it's the shape of a comet and it makes you think of a comet, because he's got six freckles on his cheek that are like the big dipper. And his face is round like the moon, too, but, gee williger, I hate astronomy. But I'd like to go to Mars just the same.

Anyway this is the way you send a smudge signal. When you get the fire started good and strong you kind of shovel it into a tin can, but if you haven't got any tin can, you don't. Scouts are supposed to be able to do without things. We should worry about tin cans. Brent Gaylong has a tin can on wheels — that's a Ford. My father says it's better to own a Ford than a can't afford. Anyway my sister says I ought to stick to my subject. Gee whiz, she must think I'm a piece of fly paper.

CHAPTER XV—THE MESSAGE

The reason that I ended that chapter was because I had to go to supper. So now I'll tell you about the signal. If we had only had a tin can with some kind of a cover to lay over it, it would have been easy. But we hadn't any so this is the way we did. After the fire was burning up we piled some of the damp grass and stuff on top of it and that made a smudge that went way up in the air. I guess any one could see that smudge maybe fifty miles, especially on account of it being up on the top of a mountain.

I said, "All we need now is a cloth or something to spread over it so we can divide the letters." Because you know we use the Morse code.

So Brent said we could have his mackinaw jacket and he sent Pee-wee down to the brook to soak it in the water so that it wouldn't catch fire. That was the beginning of Brent Gaylong's bad luck. Crinkums, that fellow must have been born on a Friday—anyway, he was born on a Friday that day, I guess. But one good thing about Friday, it's the day before Saturday. That's why there are fifty-two Good Fridays.

So then we sent the message. The first word was Uncle, so to spell that we let the smudge rise for just a second, then laid Brent's jacket over it for about three seconds, then let it rise for another second, then waited about three seconds more and then let it rise for, oh, I guess about ten seconds, maybe. That made two dots and a dash in the Morse code and it made the letter U good and big, cracky, bigger than you could make it on any blackboard, as big as the whole sky. Maybe it wouldn't mean anything to you, but that's because you're not a scout. But anyway it meant U. I don't mean it meant you, but I mean it meant U.

After that we made the other letters in the word Uncle—N-K-L-E—I don't mean K, I mean C.

Then after we'd waited about a minute so as to separate the words we spelled T-O-M, and after that there was a big blot on our writing (that's what Rossie said), because Brent's mackinaw jacket burned up. He said he was sorry, because there were some peanuts in one of the pockets.

Anyway he said he was willing to die for the cause, so he took off his khaki shirt and after Pee-wee went down and soaked it in the brook, we used that to separate the words and letters. Maybe you'll say that kind of writing isn't very neat but we knew that it could be seen for miles and miles and that if the boy scouts in Grumpy's Cross-roads saw it and read it, they'd tell Major Grumpy and he'd say the scouts were all right. Because that was our idea, we wanted those other scouts to get the credit.

I guess maybe it took a half an hour to send that message and it didn't look much like a message to us. You've got to get away off if you want to read a smudge signal. A smudge signal is no good for a fellow that's near-sighted. When we were all finished, this is what we had printed in the sky:

Uncle Tom show will be given as announced.

Deny rumors.

Boy Scouts of America.

Pee-wee wanted to put in something about foiling the railroad strikers, but Brent said if we made the message any longer he wouldn't have any clothes left. Harry said that if the scouts at Grumpy's Cross-roads got that message and delivered it to old Grump, that old Grump would surrender unconditionally. So maybe we had done a good turn for all we knew. Even if the telegraph operator at Grumpy's Cross-roads should see that smudge he'd read the message, all right. But we said that more likely he'd he asleep and that scouts are always up early because up at Temple Camp Uncle Jeb Rushmore (he's camp manager) is always telling us that the early bird catches the first worm. But, gee whiz, if I were the first worm I'd stay in bed and then the early bird wouldn't catch me.

That's what Pee-wee calls logic. That's one thing he's crazy about, — logic. Logic and Charlie Chaplin. He likes girls, too. He says they always smile at him. Gee whiz, can you blame them? It's a wonder they don't laugh out loud.

XVI — BRENT'S AMBITION

It was some job picking our way down that mountain. We could see the road and the machines away down below us and the machines looked like toy autos. Brent and Harry and Pee-wee and I were together and Brent talked a lot of that nonsense like he always does. Pee-wee had the convict's suit rolled up tight and tied with a couple of thin willow twigs. If you wet them they're just as good as cord; you can even tie them in a knot. He carried the bundle on the end of his scout staff and he had his scout staff over his shoulder. He looked so important you'd think he had just captured the convict, too.

Brent said, "That's what I call real adventure; escaping from a prison and beating it off to some lonesome mountain and being taken away in an airplane. That fellow has old Monte Cristo beaten twenty ways. Some convicts are lucky. I'd like to be that chap." That's just the way he talked.

Harry said, "You might forge a couple of checks if you happen to think of it sometime."

Brent said in that funny way of his, "If I could only be sure of escaping and being carried off by an airplane. But it would be just my luck to — to — —"

"Languish," Pee-wee shouted; "that's what they do in jails — languish."

"And just serve out my term studying logic," Brent said. "But if I thought there'd be a chance to escape, I think I'd — let's see, I think I'd — what do you think of counterfeiting, Harry?"

"Burglary's better," Harry said.

"It's the dream of my life to be a convict," Brent kept up. "These little crimes don't amount to anything; what I'd like to do is to hit the high spots, get sent up for life, and then escape in a boat or an airplane. Somebody could send me a file or a saw in a bunch of flowers. What do you say? This convict is having the time of his life. That's the life — being a fugitive."

Harry said, "Well, I hope you get your wish."

Pee-wee said, "You're crazy, that's what I say."

I said, "Gee whiz, there's fun enough making a cross country trip in four autos and running into a stranded Uncle Tom's Cabin Company with bloodhounds and everything, without being sent to jail."

Brent said, "Well, I can't help it; that's the way I feel. I envy that convict. I long to languish in a dungeon cell and file away the bars in the dead of night and kill three keepers and escape in an airplane. That's living."

"Good night," I said, "not for the three keepers."

Harry said, "Well, all things come round to him that waits. My ambition is to be wrecked at sea. How about you, Roy?"

I said, "My ambition is to foil old Major Grumpy and make him fall for the scouts."

"No pep to it," Brent said; "a dark and dismal dungeon with rats poking around on the stone floor, that's my speed."

Cracky, that fellow's awful funny.

"You'd never get any dessert," Pee-wee shouted.

Brent said, "Who wants dessert when he can get a crust of bread and a mug of water?"

"I do," the kid shouted. "I want two helpings."

That was his ambition.

XVII – A SIDE SHOW

Pretty soon you'll see why I named this chapter "A Side Show." When we got down to the road all those show people were sitting around on the rocks talking and laughing and telling Westy lots of funny adventures that they had had. Oh, boy, if I wasn't a boy scout I'd like to be in an Uncle Tom's Cabin Company, that's one sure thing. That's my ambition. Jails and dungeons may be all right, I'm not saying, but anyway, I'd like to be in a show – especially one that gets stranded. They said that they could see the signal away up on the mountain, and the man that had to beat Uncle Tom, he was an awful nice man, he said he could read most all of it because he used to be a telegraph operator. But he said he liked beating Uncle Tom better. Uncle Tom said he didn't mind being beaten once a day but he didn't like matinees.

Now I'm going to tell you about how we all got separated together – that's what Pee-wee said. When we were all ready to go, Harry couldn't start the engine of the van. He said, "Brent, I wish you'd take a squint at this motor; it heats up and the water boils over."

Brent said, "I think the timer must have been set by Pee-wee's watch." Pretty soon he said he guessed it was just a short circuit.

"Anyway, that's better than a long one," Pee-wee shouted.

Pretty soon Brent said he thought the coil was running the battery down. Harry said he didn't blame the coil.

Then Brent said there was a leak of current somewhere, but that he couldn't trace it. I said, "Let one of Eliza's bloodhounds try; maybe he can trace it." He said anyway the battery was discharging; believe me, if I'd had my way I'd have discharged the whole engine.

After a while Brent got it started but he said it wasn't running right and he guessed he'd have to get two new plugs. So then we looked at our map to find out if there was a village anywhere near along that road where there might be a garage. Because Brent said there ought to be more grease in the differential, too. But mostly, he said, one of the plugs wouldn't fire the charge.

Westy said, "If the plug won't fire it, why don't you get the battery to discharge it?"

Now when we looked at our map we found that about half a mile east of that mountain a road branched off from the road we were on and went through a place named Barrow's Homestead. It didn't bother to stop at Barrow's Homestead, that road didn't, but it went on and formed a, you know, a what-do-you-call-it, a junction, with the other road three or four miles farther along. It was just a kind of a loop, that road was, so as to take in Barrow's Homestead. Only that road was pretty rough.

Brent said, "I dare say we can find a young garage at that place; there are bandits everywhere in the west. If you say so, I'll drive along that road and meet you where the roads join."

Harry said, "I guess that's the best thing to do—for the rest of us to keep to the smooth, short road with the touring cars. When we get to the junction of the two roads we'll wait for you there as long as we think it's safe to wait. If you don't show up by ten o'clock, say, we'll jog along and meet you at the Veterans' Reunion at Grumpy's Cross-roads. We don't want to run any chance of not getting these people there on time. Uncle Tom has got to be thrashed this afternoon at any cost." Then he asked Uncle Tom if he wanted a cigarette. That man was awful nice—the man that played Uncle Tom. He said he had been thrashed twice a day for three years, except on Sundays. Harry said it would be a good thing if that happened to a lot of us fellows, especially me. Anyway I'd rather be Eliza and be chased by ferocious bloodhounds. That's what Mr. Abbington called them— ferocious.

Now as soon as it was decided that Brent Gaylong should drive the van along that other road, up jumped our young hero and shouted, "I'll go with you; maybe they sell ice cream sodas at that place."

As soon as he mentioned ice cream sodas all the other fellows said they'd go—except I didn't. Because I'm not crazy about an ice cream soda. I like three or four of them though.

Harry said, "Well, it looks like a mutiny and I guess we'll have to lock every one of you in the van."

By that time, Pee-wee was up on the seat of the van and he shouted, "I wouldn't mute; I'm already here and I'm going to stay here!"

Harry said, "Nobody would ever think of the word mute in connection with you; stay where you are and we'll be glad to get rid of you, and Roy too, if he wants to go."

I said, "The pleasure is mine, I go where duty calls."

"You mean you go where ice cream sodas call," the kid shouted at me.

I said, "Well, for goodness' sake, chuck that bundle inside the van and give me a chance to sit down, will you?" Because even still he had that convict's suit close by him on the seat as if he was afraid somebody would get it away from him. "What are you going to do with it?" I said. "Hang it up in the parlor when you get home?"

So then I climbed up and chucked the bundle into the van through the little window right behind the seat. Brent sat down between Pee-wee and me, and thus we started off. That's a peach of a word—thus. For a little way we could look across to the other road and see the three touring cars filled with the Uncle Tom's Cabin people and the other fellows of my patrol. Mr. Abbington was sitting with Harry and he looked awful funny with his high hat on.

All of a sudden, good night, that bloodhound that had been up on the mountain with us came tearing across from the other road. I guess he wanted to go with us. He clambered almost up to the seat and began sniffing around Brent. I bet he liked him on account of Brent's being so crazy about adventures, hey?

Brent said, "You go back where you belong, old Snoozer. Who do you think I am? Eliza?"

Then Mr. Abbington began calling him and the dog didn't seem to be able to decide what to do.

"I hear you calling me," Brent said; "go on back, Snoozer; we'll see you later."

So then the dog went back but I guess he didn't want to. Gee whiz, you couldn't blame him. Because one thing sure, if you stick to Brent Gaylong you're pretty sure to see some fun. Believe me, that fellow's middle name is adventure. Just you wait and see.

CHAPTER XVIII—A SHOWER BATH

Brent said, "I bet Brother Abbington will be pretty hot to-day with that frock coat of his and that high hat."

I said, "It's going to be a scorcher, all right."

"Lucky for me," he said, "as long as my mackinaw and my khaki shirt have gone in the good cause."

"You should worry," I told him.

"Only I don't look very presentable," he said.

"Don't you care," I said; "we won't meet anybody along this road."

"It's the least of my troubles," he said; "what I'm thinking about is this pesky engine. It jumps like a bull-frog; I think it's got the pip."

Pee-wee said, "Some engines have the sleeping sickness and they won't go at all."

Then we all got to saying how we hoped that Harry and Rossie and Tom would get the three cars to Grumpy's Cross-roads in time so those actor people could give their show.

"Even if we're not with them," I said.

"I guess we'll be able to make connections before they get there," Brent said.

"Oh, boy, that'll be some good turn," Pee-wee said. "I bet old Grump won't be mad at the scouts any more; he'll see that they're dauntless and— something or other."

"Oh, he'll see that they're something or other," Brent said. "I never knew a scout that wasn't something or other."

"He'll see that they do good turns," the kid shouted. Gee whiz, good turns are his favorite fruit—good turns and doughnuts. Even if he had a turning lathe he couldn't turn out any more good turns.

Now maybe you know what a tornado is. Anyway, there wasn't any that day. So you don't need to worry. But all of a sudden dark clouds came and pretty soon the sky was all black and the wind was blowing like anything. I guess it was a cyclone, all right, only it decided not to come that way on account of the road being so bad.

Anyway the wind kept up and blew right in our faces and after a while Brent said, "Did you bring those old togs along, kid?"

Pee-wee said, "You mean the convict suit? It's in the van."

"Well, get me the coat and I'll slip it on," Brent told him. "We may not be able to catch the convict, but I'm blamed sure I'll catch cold."

So Pee-wee went around and into the van by the doors in back and got the convict's jacket. I guess none of us thought there was anything funny about Brent wearing it for a little while. Only I said to him, just joking like, "You wanted to be a convict, now you've got your wish."

"If my mother could only see me now," he said. "Do I look like a zebra, Pee-wee?"

We had to laugh, he looked so funny in that striped jacket; but anyway it was a pretty lonely road and we weren't likely to meet anybody.

Pretty soon we began passing houses, and Brent took the jacket off and threw it back into the van through the little window in front. In about five minutes we came to a village. I said, "Go slow or you'll run over it." The village was almose right underneath the van. The main street of that village was all black and sticky from tar and oil that they had been sprinkling on it and pretty soon we came to the sprinkler, standing still right in the middle of the road, with a couple of men near it.

We had to stop because we couldn't get past, so we just sat there on the seat, watching them. The sprinkler wouldn't work and they were trying to fix it. One man was sticking a piece of wire into all the little holes along the pipe that ran crossways at the back of the big tank.

Brent said, "They'll never fix it that way. Maybe some of those holes are clogged up, but not all of them." Then he called down to the man and said, "What seems to be the trouble? Won't she sprinkle?"

"Mixture's too gol darned thick, I reckon," one of the men called back.

"Well, it wouldn't clog up all the holes," Brent said; "probably the feed pipe is clogged up."

The man said, "Well, I don't know how we're ever going to get at that unless we take the whole bloomin' thing apart."

Then I heard Brent say, under his breath kind of, "I could fix that in five minutes."

"Then you have to do it," the kid shouted; "you have to do a good turn."

"Look and see if there isn't a turn cock on the feed pipe," Brent called down; "maybe it joggled shut. That sometimes happens on an auto."

The two men got down under the sprinkler and began looking and feeling around, but they couldn't seem to find anything. After a couple of minutes Brent climbed down and said, "Let's take a look at this." I guess they could see that he was a pretty good mechanic, all right. Anyhow they stepped out of the way and Brent crawled down under the sprinkler. He lay on his back part way underneath it and we all watched him.

"He'll find the trouble," Pee-wee said to the man; "he's head of a scout troop, he is, and he's resourceful. A scout has got to be resourceful. Don't you worry, we'll do you a good turn, all right."

The men kind of smiled, and one of them said, "All right, sonny. So yer fer doin' good turns, hey?"

"Sure," Pee-wee said; "that's one of our rules. If anybody's in trouble we've got to help them out—no matter how much trouble it is. You see a scout can always help you out, because he's resourceful."

One of those men said, "Oh, that's it, is it?"

"Sure," the kid shouted; "all you have to do is come to us. Even Uncle Sam came to us when he wanted to sell Liberty Bonds; we helped him out."

The man said, "I bet he was tickled to death."

I said to Pee-wee, "Shut up; don't be shouting so much about good turns. Actions speak louder than words."

"Words speak loud enough," the kid yelled.

"Good night, you said it," I told him.

"Even now we're doing a good turn," the kid shouted; "we've got three more autos over on the other road and we're taking some Uncle Tom's Cabin actors to the Veteran's Reunion. We should worry if the railroad trains don't run."

Jimmies, I don't know how much more he might have told them, he's a human billboard for the Boy Scouts of America, that kid is; but all of a sudden, zip goes the fillum, that black tarry stuff came shooting out from all the holes in the sprinkler and Brent came crawling out from underneath it with his trousers and his shirt all black and sticky and his hair all mucked up with the stuff and with a big streaky smudge all over his face.

"Good night!" I shouted. "What happened?"

"I found it," he said; "it had joggled shut, just as I thought. If you happen to have a few feathers handy, you can tar and feather me. I did a good turn, only I didn't turn over and get out quick enough."

Oh, boy, that fellow was a sight!

XIX — BRENT GETS HIS WISH

One thing about those men, they weren't very good scouts, I'll say that much. The only good turn they did was to turn around and drive away. Maybe the Union wouldn't let them do good turns; Unions have got no use for good turns.

First we decided that we'd stop at the nearest house, but one thing about scouts, they don't like to ask for help unless they have to. But if you offer them something to eat it's all right for them to take it.

I said to Brent, "Well, you were crazy for an adventure, now you've got one."

He said, "I don't care about such a sticky one. I'm not exactly what you would call crazy about tar shower baths."

"You'll have to cut your hair off, that's one sure thing," I told him; "you'll never be able to get that stuff out of your hair."

"I'd like to sit down, too," he said; "but if I did, I could never get up again. I think the sooner I'm fixed up the better. Let's run the van alongside the road and get inside and see what we can do. Our friend's suit of clothes is still in there. After boasting about my dreams of adventure it seems rather tame to go into somebody's back kitchen for repairs. I'm afraid Harry would indulge in a gentle smile."

"He'd indulge in a gentle fit if he saw you now," I told him.

"I say let's not go to anybody for assistance," Pee-wee spoke up. "We can get gasoline out of the tank, so you can wash the tar off your face, and I've got a folding scissors in my scout knife. I'll cut your hair for you."

"How would you like to have it cut?" I asked him, just kidding him.

"I think I'd like it cut dark," he said.

I said, "Well, we'll cut it short and then if you don't like it we'll cut it longer."

So we decided that we wouldn't depend on anybody but would act just the same as if we were on a desert island where there weren't any barbers and bathtubs and things, because Columbus and Daniel Boone didn't have barbers and bathtubs and things.

"They depended upon their own initials," Pee-wee said.

"You mean initiative," I told him.

He said, "What's the difference?"

So then I ran the machine over to the side of the road right close to a kind of a grove and we got some gas out of the tank and Brent and I went inside the van. We told Pee-wee to stay outside so as to keep people from opening the doors or fooling with the car, because we were in the village and we thought maybe people would be hanging around.

There was only one thing to do with Brent's hair, and that was to cut it off, because the tar was so thick there that the gasoline wouldn't melt it. I made a pretty good job of it with the little folding scissors in Pee-wee's scout knife. We managed to get most of the tar off his face with the gasoline, but it left his face kind of all black and sooty looking.

He couldn't sit down or lean against anything on account of the tar all over his clothes, so he took them off and I handed them out to Pee-wee and told him to throw them in the grove. Then Brent put on the convict's suit, and he looked awful funny in it with his dirty face and his hair all cut short.

He said, "At last the dream of my young life has come true; I am a criminal. The only thing is I haven't committed my crime yet."

I said, "Oh, you needn't be in any hurry about that."

He said, "But it seems sort of false for me to be wearing a convict's suit when I haven't committed any crime. It seems like deceiving people. It troubles my conscience. And I haven't really escaped either. What would you do if you were me? I don't want to disgrace the uniform I wear. I wish I could think of some nice easy crime. I feel nice and clean in these things, anyway. But my conscience is black. Do you suppose there's a bank in this burg, and a jail? I was thinking if I could just let myself down by a rope. Only it would be just my luck to have a cell on the ground floor."

I said, "The best cell for you is right in this little old van, at least till we get out of town. You leave the rope business to Douglas Fairbanks. If anybody in this place should see you, good night, Sister Anne! And it isn't any joke, either. Now you've got your wish, you'll see it isn't going to be as much fun as you thought it was."

Brent sat down on an old grocery box that we had inside the van, and, jiminetty, I had to laugh, he had such a funny way about him. He looked awful tough, sort of, without his hair. He said, "Well, I appoint you my keeper. I hope I'm not such a cheap sort of a criminal as to try to escape from a delivery van. A stone dungeon or nothing for me." Gee whiz, that fellow's particular.

Just then the plot grew thicker—oh, boy! One of the doors of the van opened and Pee-wee squeezed in. He had a big piece of paper in his hand. He said, "I went up the road a little way—shh!"

I said, "I thought it was kind of quiet outside."

He said, "Shh, look at this; it was tacked to a tree. We're in desperate peril——"

Brent said, "In which?"

"Read this," the kid whispered. "I didn't see it till after I threw the clothes away and they floated down the brook. Dangers thicken—look at this." He got those words out of the movies, dangers thicken.

Brent and I read the printing on the paper and this is what it said:

ONE THOUSAND DOLLARS REWARD

Offered for information leading to the recapture of Mike Donovan, alias Rinky, escaped from Indiana State Prison. Was serving term of fifteen years for burglary and child murder. Slender of stature. Five feet nine inches in height. Is supposed to have relations in the east. Age about nineteen. Is known to be a desperate character, having served terms in New York and Pennsylvania for burglary and highway robbery.

There was some more, about who to notify and all that, but I can't remember the rest. Brent took the paper from me and sat there on the grocery box in the dim light with the doors closed, reading it. It seemed awfully dark and secret, kind of, in there.

He said, "Larceny, child murder, burglary, and highway robbery. That isn't so bad, is it? That's really more than I expected. I haven't lived in vain."

"You'll live in a jail, that's where you'll live," Pee-wee whispered. "What are we going to do?"

"You ought to know," I told him, "a scout is resourceful."

CHAPTER XX — WE CONSIDER OUR PREDICAMENT
(THAT'S PEE-WEE'S HEADING)

I said to Brent, "Now you've killed a child and highway-robbed people and broken into houses, I hope you're satisfied."

"And larcenied," the kid shouted.

"Shut up," I told him; "do you want the whole town to hear you? It's bad enough as it is; suppose somebody should come walking into this van."

Brent said, in that crazy way of his, "Boys, this is the end of an evil career. This is what comes of getting mixed up with the boy scouts. See where it has brought me. Never again will I do a good turn."

"You're crazy," Pee-wee shouted.

"Shh," I told him; "have a heart. Do you want to get us all pinched?"

"It was about the best turn I ever did," Brent said; "I turned the stop-cock all the way open. And here I am a prisoner in a dry goods delivery van with boy scouts for keepers. I'd be ashamed to look an honest burglar in the face." Honest, that's just the crazy way he talked. He said, "Now the question is to escape. I want to escape in a way that's full of pep."

Pee-wee said, "You make me tired. Do you mean to say that good turns — —"

"Will you shut up about good turns, and listen?" I said.

"I mean to say that a good turn is the cause of my downfall," Brent said; "and I wish I had a cigarette. Boys, take a lesson from my terrible example and don't ever do a good turn."

"What are you talking about?" the kid shouted.

"Shh," I told him; "keep still, will you? The first merry-go-round you see you can get on it and do all the good turns you want, only keep still and give us a chance to see where we're at, will you?"

"It's printed on the National Headquarters' letterheads," he said, "to do a good turn— —"

"It's bad advice to give a young boy," Brent said.

I said, "Keep still, you're worse than he is. Give me a chance to think, will you?"

"Roosevelt's name and Taft's name are on that letterhead," the kid began, "so that shows— —"

"I'm surprised that they should give such advice to young boys," Brent said. "I wonder if I could escape from this van with a file and let myself down with a rope?" Then he picked up a can opener and said, "Ha, ha, just the thing."

I said, "Will you please keep still a minute, both of you? Maybe you've heard the scout motto, 'Be Prepared.' That's just as important as good turns. How are we going to get away from this town? That's the question. You and your crimes, and Pee-wee and his good turns, make me tired. We've got to look facts in the face."

Brent said, "I'm ashamed to look even a fact in the face."

"Well," I told him, "you'll be looking a sheriff in the face if you don't talk in a whisper, and maybe you'll find it isn't so pleasant being arrested."

Brent said, "I'm not thinking about being arrested, I'm thinking about escaping."

"Well, you can't escape from a dry goods van," I told him.

He said, awful sad, kind of, "I know it. Oh, if I were only Eliza and could be pursued by ferocious bloodhounds."

I said, "Well, you can't have everything. You've done pretty well so far."

"Sure you have," Pee-wee whispered; "there's one of those notices tacked up in the Post Office, and everybody is talking about that fellow escaping. I told them that often boy scouts find missing people. I was telling them about good turns, and I said we'd be on the lookout."

"I hope they won't look in" Brent said.

"What else did you tell them?" I asked him, good and scared. Because I knew that if our young hero had been able to round up an audience in the Post Office, most likely he had given them the whole history of the Boy Scouts of America and a lot of other stuff besides.

"I was telling them about good turns," he said. "There was an old lady there and I carried a big bundle out to her carriage for her."

"And that's all you told them?" I asked him.

"I told them we were going to the Veterans' Reunion at Grumpy's Cross-roads," he said.

I said, "Did anybody ask you any questions?"

"Sure," he said; "a man asked me if I liked gumdrops. He gave me a bag of them. Want one?"

"Well," I said, "the best thing for us to do is to get out of this place as quick as we can. When we once strike open country, we'll be all right and when we meet the rest of the crowd we can scrape up some civilized duds."

"I wonder how I'd look in Brother Abbington's plug hat just now," Brent said.

"You should worry," I told him; "you look bad enough already."

"Speaking of plug hats," he said, "don't forget we have to get a couple of plugs for the motor. What place is this, anyway?"

"It's the place we were looking for," Pee-wee said; "it's Barrow's Homestead. There aren't any scouts here, but I told the people all about them. They're going to start a troop."

I said, "Well, it's time to start this troop if we don't want to get into trouble. This is a pretty risky business."

XXI — GETTING STARTED

As soon as I heard that Pee-wee had been in the Post Office talking, I decided that we had better get away from that place just as soon as we possibly could, if not sooner. Even Brent said he guessed the best way to escape was inside the van; he said it was more comfortable and convenient. He said the good old times when people used to escape from towers and be pursued by ferocious bloodhounds weren't any more except in the movies. He said he was discouraged.

Gee whiz, when I looked at him sitting there on that grocery box with his face all grimy and his hair cropped and that striped suit on him, I just had to laugh. I have to admit he's awful funny, that fellow is.

I said, "Well, one thing, it's mighty lucky I know how to drive a car and I can get us out of this village. And another thing, it's mighty lucky we're still just where the village begins; if we weren't we'd be surrounded. If we can get past the Post Office, we're safe."

So then Pee-wee and I tore down the signs we had outside the van about going all the way from Klucksville to New York, because people would wonder at fellows our age doing that when there was no big fellow with us. Safety first, that's what I said.

"If they think we're only going as far as Grumpy's Cross-roads," I said, "I guess nobody'll be suspicious."

Pee-wee said, "Yes, but how about Jolly & Kidder's name, and New York printed all over the sides of the van?"

"A scout is resourceful," I told him; "let's tear down the canvas from inside and be quick about it."

Now inside that van was lined with canvas to keep things from getting scratched, I guess. Brent said it was a padded cell. So we took that down and tacked it up outside on both sides so that all the printing was covered. After we did that we closed the doors of the van and locked the padlock and Pee-wee took the key. Brent called out to us that we should take a lesson by his terrible example. Then we could hear him kind of muttering, "I will escape; I will foil you all yet." Honest, he's crazy, that fellow is.

Pee-wee and I sat down on the back step for about half a minute to make up our minds what we should say if any one stopped us and asked us questions. "Anyway," he said, "that canvas on the sides will make people suspicious with no printing on it."

I said, "Well, we're not going to print any lies on it, anyway."

He said, "We don't have to print lies. Truth is stranger than fiction — that's what it said in a movie play I saw."

Then, all of a sudden he out with a piece of chalk that he always carries so as he can make scout signs and he sprawled all over one side of the van,

BOY SCOUTS

EN ROOT TO SOLDIERS' REUNION

OUR MOTTOES:

BE PREPARED

DO A GOOD TURN DAILY

I said, "That isn't the way to spell en route. What's the matter with you?"

I guess he was thinking about root beer, hey?

XXII — SILENCE!

I said to Pee-wee, "Now all we have to do is to go straight about our business and keep our mouths shut and we'll get out of this burg all right. Just keep silence. Nobody's going to stop us as long as people don't get suspicious. I can drive the car till we get out of town and I don't think any one will stop me. All you have to do is to keep silence."

"How long do I have to keep it?" he wanted to know.

I said, "Oh, keep it till it's all used up, and then I'll give you some more. Believe me, you can't have too much of it just now."

"We'll have to use up a lot of it, hey?" he said.

"More than you ever used before," I told him.

"Anyway," he said, "an innocent man has nothing to fear."

"You got that out of the movies," I told him. "An innocent man with his hair cropped and a convict suit on has a whole lot to fear."

"Innocence is a shield," he said; "it's in my copy book."

"Yes?" I said. "Well, an enclosed van is a better shield."

"Our lips will be sealed, hey?" he said. I guess he got that out of the Dan Dauntless Series; he eats those books alive.

I felt kind of shaky driving that van, but I knew I had to do it, and if a scout has to do a thing he does it. Gee whiz, I like things that are hard — except licorice jaw breakers. You get three of those for a cent. Even I can eat those if I have to, but I like marshmallows better. I like peanut brittle too. But anyway that hasn't got anything to do with driving a car.

For maybe an eighth of a mile there weren't any houses, because where we stopped was really on the edge of the village. Anyway that village didn't have much of an edge to it. Pretty soon the houses began to get near together. I guess they were always just as near together but they — you know what I mean.

Pee-wee didn't say a word; he just sat straight up beside me like a little tin soldier. It was a shame to see him wasting so much silence.

Pretty soon we came to the Post Office. There were a lot of people standing around the Post Office and they were talking about the railroad strike. I knew that if we once got past the Post Office we'd be all right. Because post offices in the country are where sheriffs and constables and other people that haven't got anything to do hang out. It wasn't much of a post office. I guess they called it a post office because there was a post out in front of it. There was one of those signs tacked to that post.

I said to Pee-wee, "This is a young reviewing stand. Look straight ahead, keep your mouth shut, and look kind of careless—you know—carefree."

Good night, you should have seen the look he put on!

"Is that what you call care free?" I whispered to him. "You look like an advertisement for tooth powder."

"That's the scout smile," he whispered.

Honest, you'd have laughed to see him; he was looking straight ahead and grinning all over his face.

"Look natural," I whispered to him. "Look as if there wasn't a convict in the van. Look as if you never saw a convict."

"How can any fellow look as if he never saw a convict?" he whispered. "Most everybody has never seen a convict."

"Well, look like them, then," I told him. "Look the same as a person would look if he wasn't helping a convict to escape."

He put on another kind of a smile and then he whispered to me, "I bet now those people will say I'm not helping a convict to escape, hey?"

"Sure," I told him; "you look as if you were on the track of an ice cream soda. Keep still and the worst will soon be over."

XXIII — FIXING IT

As we went past the Post Office I felt pretty shaky, because there were a whole lot of people there and some of them were women, and there were a lot of children, too. The women said, "Isn't he cute?" They meant Pee-wee.

Everybody stared at us as we went by, and read the printing on the van and said how the boy scouts were all right. It didn't seem as if anybody was suspicious at all. Some of them waved to us and we waved back and I heard a man say that we were lively youngsters. Gee whiz, nobody ever accused us of being dead, that's one sure thing.

One lady said how she had seen Pee-wee in the store and how he had told her all about good turns. She said it must be great to be a boy. Gee whiz, she said something that time.

"Now you see," Pee-wee whispered; "it's good I was in that store. It's good I told them all about the scouts, because now they're not suspicious. They think it's all right for kids to be doing this, because I told them scouts are resourceful."

"Did you tell them how we have plenty of initials?" I asked him.

"Do you know what safe conduct is?" he asked me.

"I know that yours isn't always safe," I told him.

"It means when a general promises not to interfere with anybody, even an enemy. He gives them safe conduct; that means that they can go ahead and not worry about being pinched, see? These people gave us safe conduct and they're not bothering us, because they know the scouts are all right. It's on account of the way I talked to them. I came along first like a kind of a — you know — a what-d'ye-call-it — — "

"I don't know what to call it," I said.

"A herald," he blurted out.

"Well," I said, "you look more like the funny page in the Journal to me. Don't talk too loud, the danger isn't passed."

By that time we had got about fifty yards past the Post Office and I was feeling kind of nervous, but just the same I knew the danger was over.

Pee-wee said, "Do you mean to tell me that those people would let a couple of kids like us go by driving a big van, and never ask them any questions, if they didn't know that we were all right? I fixed it all right, while you and Brent were worrying your lives out in the van. Now we're safe."

I said, "Oh, you're the little fixer, all right."

Just then, good night, one of those men came running after us calling, "Hi thar, wait a minute, you youngsters!"

Oh, boy, a cold shudder ran down my back. I said, "We're pinched. I knew it was too good to be true."

I stopped the car and when the man caught up with us he said, all out of breath, "What's this here talk one of you youngsters were givin' us 'baout good turns? Allus ready ter do a favor, as I understand?"

Oh, bibbie, wasn't I relieved.

"That's our middle name," Pee-wee said.

"Wall then, haow abaout doin' one naow?" the man said.

By that time there were about a dozen people standing around in the road and I gave Pee-wee a nudge and said, "Watch your step; let me do the talking."

But he didn't pay any attention to me. Off he went with a lot of stuff out of the handbook and wound up by saying how scouts were supposed to help strangers. "Sure, we'll do anything you want," he said; "all you have to do is to ask us."

"Wall then," the man said, "here's a lot of folks wantin' to go to the reunion at the Crossroads and we was thinkin' as haow you might pack 'em inter this here van of yourn as long as the trains ain't runnin'."

Jumping jiminies! I nearly fell through the seat.

XXIV—SNOOZER SETTLES IT

That was a home-run all right I said, all flabbergasted. "You see, the only trouble is I'm not an experienced driver and these are—they're pretty rough roads—and—eh—"

"That's one thing about us," Pee-wee piped up; "we're not as smart as we look. Maybe it seems as if we could do most anything, but we can't. That's one thing about a scout, he has to admit it if he doesn't know everything. He has to—he has to—eh—he has to safeguard the lives of others. See? Suppose we ran into a ditch and upset the car and everybody got killed. They wouldn't thank us, would they?"

One of the ladies said, "Oh, isn't he just too funny for anything!"

The man said, kind of slow and drawly like, he said, "Wall, yer could drive slow en' thar ain't no ditches."

"Even one ditch would be enough," the kid said. "Isn't there just one?"

Jiminetty, I could hardly keep a straight face. There were all those people crowding around the van and saying how nice it would be if we would take a group to the reunion and how we had plenty of room. I thought of Brent sitting on the grocery box inside, and I bet he was laughing.

I said under my breath to Pee-wee, "All right, you got us into this with your good turns; now you can get us out."

Then a man said, "A couple of boys who are going to have an eye out to recapture a convict, like this here little feller says, they ought to be smart enough and kind enough, I reckon, to give some of these here disappointed souls a lift. Jest you boys open these here doors and let the youngsters pile in, so they can go see Uncle Tom's Cabin."

"That—that show isn't going to be much good," Pee-wee said; "and I can tell you one thing, it's pretty stuffy in that van. That's one thing scouts believe in—fresh air."

By that time he was fidgeting around on the seat and some of the people were laughing and some of them looked surprised.

"That's just it," Pee-wee said; "if you were boy scouts and you were going to try to capture a criminal, you wouldn't want a lot of children along, would you? And ladies? Ladies are a-scared of criminals; gee, I don't blame them."

Somebody said, "Oh, I guess the hounds they got on the trail will find the convict, all right, so you boys can jest consider if you're goin' to live up to your words or not 'baout doin' good turns."

Oh, boy, that was a terrible moment in Pee-wee's life. I guess Dan Dauntless never had so much to worry about. But that kid has some sense, anyway, and that's more than that story fellow has. In a couple of seconds I noticed that he was wiping his face with his handkerchief and I saw that he was getting the key sort of rolled up in the cloth at the same time. Then he made believe to put the handkerchief in his back pocket, but really he dropped it through the little window into the van. You couldn't even hear it drop inside.

Then he said, "The trouble is that this van is locked and we haven't got the key." That kid would never have said that while he had the key, because it would have been a lie. And scouts don't lie, that's sure.

Jiminy, I don't know what those people thought; anyway I felt pretty mean. The ladies said anyway they were just as much obliged to us. The men looked kind of as if they didn't have much use for us, but they didn't say anything and I had to admit that Pee-wee had got away with it all right.

Then, good night, Sister Anne, what should I see but our old college chum Snoozer from the Uncle Tom's Cabin show. There he was, right among all those people, pushing them out of the way and sniffing around as if he was half crazy. Pee-wee and I jumped down and pushed past the people who were all crowding around the back of the van, and, good night, there was that pesky actor dog with his feet on the step, sniffing and sniffing at the doors and barking and yelping for all he was worth.

"Chop down them doors!" I heard a man say. "That's somethin' wrong here. This here dog is an official bloodhound, and, by gum, he's tracked that thar convict. That chap paid these youngsters to help him escape, that's what he has — by thunder! Somebody get an axe out of the Post Office and chop down these here doors. Don't either one of you youngsters try to run or, by thunder, you'll drop in your tracks. Good turns, eh? So them's the kind of good turns you do, hey? Get an axe somebody — quick!"

XXV — BIG EXCITEMENT AT BARROW'S HOMESTEAD

I was kind of excited, but I said to Pee-wee, "Don't get scared; all they'll do is arrest him; he'll get off."

Then one of the men came up and said to us awful loud and gruff, "Naow, you kids, aout with that key, hand it over!"

I said, "Didn't you hear my chum say that we haven't got the key? It shows you don't know much about scouts if you think they lie. If you want to know where the key is, it's inside."

"Wall then, yer better crawl through that little winder up thar in front and git it," he said.

"I don't have to get it," I told him; "go and get it yourself if you want it. You must have been reading dime novels if you think that boys like us help convicts to escape. If you tear down those doors you'll put them up again, I'll tell you that."

Just then along came a man with a brass badge on about as big as a saucer. I said to Pee-wee, "Look what he's hiding." He had an axe, too. There were a lot of people crowding all about him. One of them said, "It's a pretty desperate attempt, Constabule." The man said, "I'll have him behind the bars in about a jiffy. These boys is accessories, that's what they are."

"Accessories are things that come with motor-boats," the kid whispered to me.

I said, "Well, we're the kind of accessories that come with motor vans. This is some circus; Brent will get his wish and go to jail, all right. There's no use getting scared."

By that time everything was excitement. People came running out of houses and crowded around the van and stared at Pee-wee and me. Gee whiz, I don't know where all the people came from. All the while the dog kept clawing at the doors of the van and barking and yelping. I wondered how Brent felt inside the van. In about five minutes the whole town was out, gaping and talking, all excited.

The constable said to us, "Naow then, you youngsters, you been compoundin' a felony, that's what you been doin'. Now who's inside that van? Who yer hidin'? Somebody, hey?"

"I'm not denying anything," I told him. "All I say is we didn't break any law."

"Wall, yer admit yer concealin' somebody in thar, ain't yer—huh?" he shouted.

I said, "I'm not denying it, but I'm not scared of you."

He said, "Yaas? Wall, we'll soon see. We'll have him under lock and key for sartin, if that's what he likes."

"That's his favorite pastime," I said; "you don't know him."

"Surraound this here wagon, you people," the constable said, "and keep a watch on these kids; they're pretty slippery."

So then the constable and another man began chopping down the doors. "It's up to them," I said to Pee-wee; "we should worry."

"What do you suppose Brent will do?" he said.

"They'll lock him up till the whole thing is explained," I said; "they won't take our word for anything. He's got troubles of his own at last; I hope he's satisfied. He wanted bread and water, now he'll get it."

"They'll lock us up, too, won't they?" the kid said, good and scared. "That man is keeping his eye on us."

All the while the dog kept yelping and clawing at the doors and the people crowded closer around so as to see better. Gee, I felt kind of sorry for Brent, because I saw he was up against it.

All of a sudden down came one of the doors and the bloodhound sprang inside and came out again. The constable poked his head in and said,

"Well, I'll be jiggered!" Pee-wee and I looked inside and, good night, that van was as empty as an ice cream soda glass when Pee-wee is through with it.

"Well—what—do—you—know—about—that?" I stammered under my breath to Pee-wee.

"His dream came true," Pee-wee whispered to me; "he kept his vow, he foiled everybody, he escaped. He—he—he what-d'ye-call-it—he hasn't lived in vain—hey?"

"He hasn't lived in the van very long, that's sure," I whispered. "He has put it all over these people and us too. Can you beat that fellow?"

"He defied locks and bolts and dungeons like Houdini," the kid said. I guess he saw Houdini in the movies.

"Sure, he's a real hero at last," I said; "but he's got me guessing."

The constable and a couple of other men were stamping around inside the van and he called out, "Thar ain't no clew here, nothin' but this here can opener." And then he came out with the can opener in his hand.

Gee whiz, I just couldn't help shouting right out in front of everybody. I said, "That clew explains the whole mystery. There was a can of baked beans in that van, and he must have opened it and emptied them out and secreted himself in the empty can. When we threw the can away, he escaped."

The constable said, "What's all this talk? I want to know who you kids is, anyway. And I want ter know what you're doin' here, runnin' this big van all by yourselves."

I said, "I'm Sherlock Nobody Holmes, the boy detective. This is my trusty pal, Scout Harris. We're on our way to kidnap Major Grumpy in this van and hold him until he gives up one thousand dollars to the Boy Scouts of America. Can you tell us where we can buy a couple of spark plugs?"

XXVI — TO THE RESCUE

All of a sudden the plot grew thicker. I thought we'd have to thin it with gasoline, it grew so thick. For a few minutes Pee-wee and I just stood there wondering what had become of Brent and laughing at the constable who was holding his axe in one hand and our can opener in the other, and all the people stood around staring at us as if they didn't know what to make of us.

The constable said, "I daon't like the looks uv this here, I don't. You allowed there was somebody in that van. Now whar is he?"

I said, "I didn't allow anything, I just didn't deny anything. What's the use of blaming us because you half chopped the van to pieces? All you've got is a can opener — we should worry. You seem to trust the dog; if you want to ask any questions you'd better ask him. The only person he knows how to track is Eliza, because that's his business."

"He's on the stage," Pee-wee piped up.

"You mean he's in the van," I said.

The constable said, "Wall, I reckon you youngsters'd better tell yer story ter Justice Cummins. It's mighty funny two young boys travelin' by theirselves in a big van."

"I'll recount our adventures to him," Pee-wee piped up. "Where is he?"

For about half a minute the constable just stood there staring at us. I guess he didn't know what he'd better do. All the rest of the people stood around, staring. I guess it was the biggest thing that ever happened in Barrow's Homestead. Inside the van a couple of men were holding the bloodhound by the collar. Some excitement.

All of a sudden, zip goes the fillum, along the road came an auto, pell-mell! It came through the village from the direction we were going in.

"Look!" Pee-wee said. "Look who's in it; it's Harry; who's that with him?"

Before I had a chance to say anything, the car was close up to us and Harry and another person were stepping out. Harry was laughing all over his face, but he was in a terrible hurry, I could see that. I gave one look at the person who was with him and began to roar.

"It's—it's Brent—Gaylong," Pee-wee whispered.

I said, "Don't make me laugh any harder or I'll die of shock."

Honest, even now when I think of it I have to laugh. He looked like Charlie Chaplin only more so. And he had such a funny way about him too—kind of dignified. He had on a great big straw hat like a farmer and a black coat like a minister, only it was all in shreds. It was his trousers that made him look like Charlie Chaplin. Laugh! They were about a hundred times too big and a mile too long, and every time he took a step he stumbled all over himself and had to hoist them up. His big hat was pulled way down over his ears and—oh, I just can't tell you about it. He was a scream. And all the while he had a very dignified, severe look on his face, even when he tripped all over himself.

Honest, I just howled. I didn't hear Pee-wee laugh; I guess he must have fainted. Harry came along behind Brent, trying not to laugh but every time Brent's feet caught in his trousers I could see Harry's face all twisted up just as if he was trying as hard as he could not to scream. Every step Brent took I thought he'd go kerflop on the ground. The people were all giggling, but he didn't notice them at all, only kept on looking very sober and stern—oh, boy, it was a scream.

He said, "What is all this?" And then he fell all over himself and gave his trousers a hitch. "Who is interfering with these boys in the performance of their duty? Stand back, everybody!" And he went staggering against a tree and gave his trousers a good hitch up. "Who is the leader of this motley throng?" That's what he said, and, gee whiz, I thought he'd skid and land on his head. You couldn't see his hands, his sleeves were so long. "Who dares to stand—" he said, and, good night, he went kerflop on the ground and got right up again. I had a headache from laughing.

Harry Donnelle just sat down on the step of the van and shook and shook.

Brent pointed at the sheriff with the floppy end of his sleeve and said, "You and your minions are charged with trespassing upon the property of Jolly & Kidder, Inc., New York. Wait till I roll up my sleeves so I can point better. Who dares to stand in the way of the Boy Scouts of America?"

"Thar's a convict missin' from araound these parts," the constable said; "who are you, anyway, and your friend thar?"

Brent said, "We represent the Archibald Abbington Uncle Tom's Cabin Company who are touring the country, drawing laughter and tears with their excruciating and heart-rending drama, and I am in search of one of our ferocious bloodhounds. We are in partnership with the Boy Scouts of America and any one attempting to interfere with our noble effort to put an end to slavery will be punished to the full extent of the law. When we have an opportunity we will endeavor to find your convict for you. Please stand aside, everybody, and allow the procession to pass."

CHAPTER XXVII—ANOTHER DISCOVERY

Brent stumbled up the step and stood in back of the van, holding his trousers up with one hand and waving the other hand in the air.

"Free ride to the Veterans' Reunion at Grumpy's Cross-roads!" he began shouting. "Children and veterans free! We take you but do not bring you back. No connection with criminals and convicts! Free ride to the carnival. Veterans welcome! All aboard for the carnival! Hail to the Grand Army of the Republic and the Boy Scouts of America. Hurrah for Jolly & Kidder, New York's great cash store! Step inside, veterans!"

Pretty soon an old man with an old blue army cap came hobbling out of the crowd, and Harry helped him up into the van. That was a starter. Men began bringing boxes from the Post Office and putting them in the van for seats. Most of the mothers wouldn't let their children go because there wasn't any way for them to get back, but the veterans didn't seem to mind that. We got three veterans in Barrow's Homestead and then started out. I don't know what the constable thought, but we should worry about that. All the people cheered us and gave us a fine send-off. Pee-wee said they were stricken with remorse—I guess he got that out of a movie play.

We stopped for a couple of spark plugs and to get the timer of the van adjusted, and a lot of the kids followed us as far as the end of the town.

Harry drove the van and Brent drove the touring car, and Pee-wee and I sat with Brent.

I said, "I wish you'd tell us about your adventures, you crazy Indian. I thought we were in for a lot of trouble in that village. You've got me guessing. Anyway you escaped like you said you were going to do. But I'd like to know where you came from and where you got that bunch of rags."

He said, "You should never laugh at honest rags. Beneath these rags beats a noble heart. Boys, I am sick of crime and I am going to reform." That's just the way he talked, the crazy Indian. He said, "I have had my fondest wish, I have been a convict—a villyan. I have languished in a dark moving van, I have foiled the shrewdest people in the world, the boy scouts — not. Would you like to hear the story of my evil career? I began life as an honest boy. I never stole but once in my life and that was when I stole second base in a ball game."

I said, "Will you stop your jollying and tell us what happened?"

He said, "Posilutely I will. There were two boy scouts sitting on the step outside the Jolly & Kidder state prison. I was inside in my convicts' stripes."

"Were you languishing?" Pee-wee piped up.

Brent said, "No, I was eating a banana. I said two scouts, but really it was only about one and a half. They were supposed to be alert, observant, resourceful."

I said, "That's right, rub it into us."

He said, "While they were arguing on the back step I stood upon a grocery box and crawled through the little window in back of the front seat. I wasfree, like Monte Carlo — I mean Monte Cristo —"

"You mean Monticello," I told him.

"You mean Montenegro," Pee-wee put in.

"The world seemed bright and new," Brent said.

"You're crazy," I told him; "go on, where did you get those clothes?"

He said, "Shh. Can I count on you never to breathe a word? The man I got these clothes from lies dead in yonder swamp."

"Who put him there?" Pee-wee wanted to know.

Brent said, "Shh, I did. The man was innocent. He was standing in a field beyond the swamp. He was doing no harm. I approached him, crawling through the grass."

"What was he doing there?" Pee-wee wanted to know.

"He was scaring away crows," Brent said.

"He was a scarecrow!" I blurted out.

"A harmless, innocent, hard working scarecrow," Brent said. "As I think of it now — —"

"You make me tired!" Pee-wee yelled. "Why didn't you say so?"

Brent said, "His trustful, happy, carefree face haunts me now. He was only scaring away the crows — —"

"You give me a pain!" the kid shouted. "You're crazy."

Brent said, "But I thought of my dungeon in the Jolly & Kidder van and of my brutal keepers, those two boy scouts — asleep on the back step. I said to myself, 'I will never return whither — —'"

"You mean thither," Pee-wee said.

"I said to myself, 'They will have to kill me to take me alive,'" Brent said.

"Anyway, you killed him?" I asked him.

He said, "I killed him in cold blood — anyway it wasn't more than lukewarm. I tore him to pieces and took his clothes and concealed my telltale convict stripes under a weeping willow. It was weeping its eyes out."

"It's a wonder it wasn't laughing," I told him.

He said, "The poor fellow was as thin as a stick; his arms were made of a cross stick, I think it was a broom stick. He lies under the marsh grass in yonder swamp. And I am free!"

"You're crazy too," the kid shouted.

"I said I would escape and I did," Brent began to laugh. "I decided that I would escape from the very people who claim to be the most alert and wide-awake — the boy scouts. You say I'm crazy. Very well, even a crazy person can foil the boy scouts. I suppose that's what you call logic."

"That's what you call nonsense," Pee-wee yelled.

"I hope you boys had a good nap while I was escaping," Brent said. "It was a shame to do it, it was so easy. I tried to leave good plain footprints, I did all that an honest convict could to help you, but in vain. I doubt if the boy scouts could trail a steam roller. As for the authorities of Barrow's Homestead ... but I've seen enough of crime and its evil results." That's just the way he talked. "Henceforth I mean to be honest."

"You're a nut, that's what you are!" Pee-wee shouted.

Brent said, awful kind of heroic like, he said, "Ha! Sayest thou so? Then glance at this paper."

I said, "What is it? Where did you get it?"

"I got it out of the inside pocket of this old coat," he said; "and it means mischief. Shh, no one has seen it but Harry Domicile; he agrees with me that it has to do with a dark plot."

"You mean you found it in the scarecrow's pocket?" Pee-wee asked him, all excited.

"I found it in the scarecrow's inside pocket," Brent said. "I don't think the scarecrow knew it was there. It is very mysterious. I think we are on the track of a new mystery. That anybody who wore a black frock coat should have had such a paper in his possession is very strange. It is no wonder the crows shunned him."

CHAPTER XXVIII – A MYSTERIOUS PAPER

Brent handed me the paper and Pee-wee nearly pushed me off the seat sticking his head way over and trying to read it. I have to admit it was mighty interesting what was on that paper. The more Pee-wee stared at it the bigger his eyes got, and it had me guessing, too.

All the while, Brent just sat there driving the machine as if he wasn't interested in the paper at all. He said, "You seem to like it. I pick up papers like that every day. If you don't care for that one, just say so and I'll dig you up another; I'll find you German spy maps, lost patent papers of wonderful inventions, mortgage papers stolen by villyans, anything you say; just say the word."

"If you don't care for this one, don't be afraid to say so. I know where there are some documents about a dark anarchist plot. Do you care about anarchist plots? Some people like them and others don't; it's just a matter of taste."

I said, "Good night, this will do for me."

Pee-wee said, all excited, "Maybe it means millions of dollars; maybe it means bars of gold. We'll solve the mystery, hey?"

"Oh, just as you say," Brent said; "you know my stand on mysteries and adventures; I eat them raw."

That paper was all old and yellow and when we opened it I had to hold it on my knee, because it tore where the creases were. I guess maybe it was as old as ten years. It looked as if it had been torn out of a memorandum book and the writing was made with a lead pencil and it was kind of blurred, but anyway, this is what it said:

Snake Creek. North shore from Ohio R. to Skeleton Cove, Top of S Cove. Follow line due north from willow. Cons to west. Stake. Measure ninety-two feet along north line, then follow line due NW through T.W. Stake. Treasure at HW limit, indicated at AN Stake. Follow S line south to pie.

Pee-wee said, very mysterious like, "What da you think it is? It tells where there's buried treasure, doesn't it?"

"Sure it does," I said. "It sounds just like the directions in the Gold Bug by Edgar Allan Poe."

"It sounds just like Treasure Island," Pee-wee put in.

Brent said, "Well, I don't know. I was thinking about it and I decided that it's a bill of fare."

"A what?" Pee-wee shouted.

"You see it's got stake and pie on it," Brent said.

"You make me tired!" the kid fairly yelled. "That paper shows where buried treasure is hidden."

Brent said, "Well then, that scarecrow must have been a pirate in his younger days. He had an evil past and I'm glad I killed him."

"You seem to think it's a joke," I said; "but it tells where there's buried treasure, that's one sure thing. You can't make anything else out of it—can you?"

Brent said, "Buried treasure's good enough for me—gold or stakes or pies, I don't care. I'd like to dig up a few buckwheat cakes just now."

"Do you know what you are? Do you know what you are?" the kid began shouting. "You're a Philippine—that's what you are!"

I said, "You mean a philistine—that's a person that makes fun of things and doesn't believe anything."

Brent said, "The only time I ever went after buried treasure I was foiled by the boy scouts. Never again. They wouldn't chop down a tree under which the treasure was buried because they loved trees."

"This isn't under a tree," Pee-wee said; "it's in a cove—on the end of a line due north. That's different. That's always the kind of a place wkere treasure is—in a cove. You can tell by the names that there's treasure there—Snake Creek and Skeleton Cove and lines due north and willows and everything. It says treasure, doesn't it? What more do you want?"

"Only where's the place?" Brent said.

"We'll find it," Pee-wee said; "we'll find it if we, if we—drop in our tracks."

Brent said, "That's something I've always longed to do—drop in my tracks. I'd like to be rescued by a St. Bernard dog."

I said, "Good night, have a heart. There are dogs enough in this series of thrilling adventures."

Brent said, "Well anyway, this is the only story of adventure that has a scarecrow for a villain. What d'ye say?"

XXIX—THE MYSTERY DEEPENS

Brent said, "Well, as long as you like my little mystery, we might as well take a peep into it. We may have a couple of hairbreadth escapes, you never can tell. By rights, we ought to quarrel over the treasure after we have found it, and all kill each other. That's the way they usually do."

"They don't do that way any more," Pee-wee said; "they divide it up."

Brent said, "No, I insist on quarreling over it."

He folded the paper and put it back in his pocket. It seemed funny for a paper like that to be in an old black frock coat like ministers wear. I had to laugh at Brent on account of the sober way he tucked it back into the pocket.

I said, "It's got me interested, that's one sure thing. But how are we going to find out where that place is?"

He said, "Well, the proper way would be for us just to fit out an expedition and go in search of it like old what's-his-name who hunted for the soda fountain down in Florida."

Pee-wee said, "Ponce de Leon, he hunted for the Fountain of Youth."

"But the best way," Brent said, "if you're really interested, is for us to get hold of a map of the Ohio River when we hit Indianapolis. We cross the Ohio at Wheeling and if that old creek is anywhere in our neighborhood we'll see if we can hoe up a few nuggets. That's the proper thing, isn't it— nuggets?"

"Nuggets and pieces of eight," Pee-wee said, very serious.

Brent said that we had enough on our minds then, with the Uncle Tom's Cabin people and the Veterans' Reunion, and that we'd better get along, especially as Harry with the van had almost caught up to us.

But one more thing happened before we got very far from Barrow's Homestead, and it threw some light on the mystery—that's what Pee-wee said. A man in a pair of overalls came along the road and Brent stopped to ask him a couple of questions. While the machine was standing there, the van passed us. Gee, there were a lot of people in it and on it and all over.

Harry said, "Do you want us to tow you? Come on, hurry up, you'll be late for the show. We've got Sherman's march through Georgia beat a hundred ways."

Brent said, "Don't bother us, we're chasing after nuggets." Then he said to the man, "You don't happen to know who owns that land beyond the marsh down at the other end of town, do you? Before you get to the Post Office? There's a big cornfield there."

I whispered to Pee-wee, "Keep your mouth shut, now, and don't tell him about good turns."

The man said, "Yer mean swamp acres? That's part o' th' old Deacon Snookbeck place."

Brent said, "Yes. Who's he?"

"Wa'l, he ain't," the man said, "but he was. Th' best thing I can say abaout that ole codger is, he's dead."

Brent rested his arms on the steering wheel and talked kind of careless, sort of. He said, "I was just wondering if the place was for sale. So he was a queer ole codger, the deacon, hey?"

The man said, "Yes, en' more'n that as I've heared tell. I guess young Snookbeck ain't calc'latin' on sellin' th' place. I reckon nobody raound these parts is wantin' ter buy it, neither. Yer see thar was a kind of a mystery 'baout ole Ebenezer. Some folks even say his haouse is haunted by a chap he murdered. But I reckon he wasn' as bad as all that."

Oh, boy, you should have seen Pee-wee! He just sat there staring, his eyes as big as dinner plates. He didn't say a word, only just stared.

Brent said, "House of mystery, hey? The Frock-coated Villyan! That would be a good name for a photoplay, huh?"

That man leaned his elbow on the side of the car and said, kind of friendly like, as if we were special friends of his, he said, "Wa'l, 'baout, let's see, nigh onter ten year ago, thar was a couple of young chaps wearin' khaki like you chaps, come out this way en they wuz rootin' raound on th' deacon's farm. They weren't plantin', that was sure; and they weren't no farm hands. Nobody seemed jest able ter find out ezactly what they were, 'cause they never talked ter nobody. Aunt Josie Anne, daown th' road a piece, asked one uv 'em who he thought he was. He said he thought he was Santa Claus, but he wasn' sure. They wuz kind o' comics, both uv 'em. Wa'l, I ain't ashamed ter tell no man who I am."

Brent said, "You're right," just sort of to encourage him to talk.

The man said, "Wa'l, they stayed at th' deacon's house 'n' one night they wuz out with a lantern in the middle of the night, under the big tree near th' deacon's haouse. Steub Berry, he 'laowed they wuz buryin' treasure thar. Some folks had it them two strangers wuz Mexican spies 'n' others reckoned they wuz army deserters. Th' ole deacon, he jes' laughed and said we couldn' guess. He wouldn' deny nuthin'. All of a sudden, ker-bang, they disappeared jes' like that 'n' some folks said th' deacon murdered both uv 'em ter git th' treasure. My wife, she allus had it, they come off some ranch or other with a lot uv stealin's. Wa'l, 'twas a nine days' wonder 'n arter that folks kinder fought shy of th' deacon."

Brent said, "And he's dead now?"

"Oh, deader'n a mummy," the man said. "When the world war come some folks said as haow that pair might a been German spies all th' while, kind uv studying 'raound. But young Snookbeck he says if old Ebenezer had anything hid it would be in his Bible, en' 's long 's 'tain't thar, 'tain't nowhere. But that's treasure hid somewhere, I say, 'cause them wuz mighty funny doin's of them strangers. Yer goin' ter th' reunion over t' 'he Cross-roads?"

CHAPTER XXX—WE MAKE A PROMISE

As soon as we had started, Brent said, "Well, it doesn't look half bad, does it?"

"Do you know who those fellows were? Do you know who those fellows were?" our young hero fairly screamed.

"I think they came from Mars," Brent said; "that's the way it looks to me."

I said, "You can joke but it's pretty serious."

"They were smugglers that's what they were," Pee-wee shouted.

"They were either smugglers or book-agents," Brent said. "In either case they deserved to be murdered. Maybe they were introducing a new kind of soap— —"

"You make me sick," Pee-wee yelled; "there's treasure somewhere and we're going to find it! It's at HW limit, it said so, HW means something abouthollow well, I bet you."

Brent said, "Maybe it means hot waffles; there's a whole table d'hote dinner in that paper. Maybe it means Hamburger wheat cakes. Anyway, the Ohio River is a long way from Barrow's Homestead."

Then Brent got kind of serious, not very serious, but kind of serious—as serious as he could. And he said we should promise him that we wouldn't think any more about that dark, mysterious paper, or talk about it to the other fellows until we got all through at Grumpy's Crossroads and reached Indianapolis so he could get hold of a map. Because if we couldn't find any stream named Snake Creek running into the Ohio River, he didn't want the fellows to be disappointed. He said there was no use of our going on a wild goose chase.

You can bet we kept our promise to Brent, but I guess Pee-wee didn't have any more sleep till we reached Indianapolis. But anyway, he had a pretty good appetite. He buried some treasure every night—ice cream sodas at the reunion.

That's one thing I like about slavery. Because if there hadn't been any slavery there wouldn't have been any Civil War, and if there hadn't been any Civil War there wouldn't have been any Veterans' Reunion, and if there hadn't been any Veterans' Reunion, there wouldn't have been any ice cream sodas there. See?

Gee whiz, I never was in the Civil War, or the uncivilized war or any other kind, but I got a black eye once. Anyway, I killed four sodas when I got to that reunion.

I did it for my country's sake.

CHAPTER XXXI—WE REACH OUR DESTINATION

Now maybe you'll say it was a long time since we left those other cars and the rest of the fellows, but it was only about an hour. Only a lot happened in that hour—it was condensed, like. That's the way I like things. Only I don't like condensed milk. But I wish they had condensed ice cream. Pee-wee's a condensed scout. I'd like to have condensed lessons, too. Anyway my sister likes pickles—gee, I hate them. She says even a postage stamp can stick to its subject better than I can. I should worry. I told her you could send an animal by mail, because once I saw a letter with a seal on it. She's all the time sending notes to Harry Donnelle, she is. She gets awful mad when I jolly her. She plays the mandolin.

Let's see, where was I? Oh, yes, now I know. Pretty soon (she likes bonbons too), pretty soon the van and our car came to the place where the two roads what-d'ye-call-it—converge—that means come together. And, gee whiz, we had a young reunion right there. Mr. Abbington was awful nice, but, oh boy, he could hardly keep that other bloodhound from chewing Brent all to pieces. I guess he thought he was a tramp.

Harry said, "Ladies and gentlemen, allow me to introduce the Scarecrow of Barrow's Homestead. The only one in captivity. We intend to exhibit him at the reunion for the small sum of a dime, ten cents—three cents' war tax. He used to be an escaped convict, but now he's reformed and he's a respectable scarecrow, the only real scarecrow ever exhibited. The crows drop dead when they see him."

Gee whiz, you ought to have heard Miss Ophelia and Topsy laugh. Even little Eva, she laughed. I guess she forgot that she was going to die and go to Heaven. Anyway, she was awful happy. Gee, Brent made them all laugh.

I bet you think it was a crazy procession that started off for Grumpy's Cross-roads, but what cared we? Gee whiz, if you don't like it you know what you can do.

92

There was Harry driving the van that was chock full of veterans, because they had picked up some along the road, and those veterans couldn't even have gone if the railroads had been running, because they lived too far away from stations and they had never been to things like that before.

Harry made all the Uncle Tom's Cabin people wear their costumes and when we got near to Grumpy's Cross-roads he had the cruel villyan stand on top of the van cracking his whip. But anyway Uncle Tom sat beside me, eating peanuts, and he should worry. Brent looked awful funny, driving one of the touring cars, but that only made it funnier.

After about two hours more we came to Grumpy's Cross-roads. They were pretty cross, all right, because there was a sign that said:

AUTOMOBILE LAWS STRICTLY ENFORCED

Oh, boy, you just ought to have seen us. The big van went first, with the man with the whip up on top, holding the ferocious bloodhounds. Next came Rossie's car full of veterans and then the other two cars full of those actor people all dressed up for their play.

We rolled into the Main Street and a band that was there, just getting ready to go to the parade ground, I guess, marched in front of us and played "Peggy." Inside of ten seconds there were people crowding all around us, but Harry told them to get out of the way, he didn't care who they were— constables, sheriffs, judges, or anything.

"Where's the parade ground?" he shouted.

A man called, "Who are you, anyway? Whar do you come from?"

Gee whiz, it gave me a good thrill when I heard Harry shout back, "We're the Boy Scouts of America, that's who we are! Friends and comrades to the boys who were chased off the parade ground. And the show opens at 3 P. M. sharp, so get your tickets and buy your peanuts! We're here! And not all the railroads in the country can stop us. On the job, that's our motto! Get from under if you don't want to be run down. There's only one man in this whole country we'll take any orders from and that's Major Grumpy!"

CHAPTER XXXII—SURRENDER AND INDEMNITY

Gee whiz, we reminded ourselves of General Pershing coming home. Just before we drove into the parade ground, a little fellow about as big as Pee-wee came running up and called to us. He was all excited. He shouted, "We read your signal; we saw it way up on the mountain. People said it was just the woods on fire but we knew what it meant; we read it. We've got a signaler in our patrol. But Major Grumpy said it was just the woods on fire."

Harry shouted down to him, "Climb up on the band wagon and be quick about it if you want to be in at the finish. Where's the rest of your bunch?"

Pee-wee said, "Troop, not bunch; don't you know anything about the scouts?"

Harry said, "Excuse me, I mean gang."

That kid said that most of them were peeking through the fence of the parade grounds, because they had been chased out. He said one of them went in to tell Major Grumpy about the smudge message and that he had been chased out again. He said they had dandy ice cream cones in there; he said the ice cream went way down into the point. Oh, boy, that's the kind I like. He said that one of them had enough ice cream in it for two fellows; gee, I've never seen any like that. But I've seen fellows that have room enough for two cones.

Poor little kid, he didn't have any scout suit or anything—only just a scout hat.

Harry said, awful nice and friendly sort of, he said, "Well, you just climb up here. So you read that message, hey? Well, you and your outfit are all right, Kiddo."

"Not outfit!" Pee-wee yelled.

Harry said, "Excuse me, I mean sewing circle."

I guess that kid thought Harry was crazy; anyway we don't need anybody to tell us we're crazy, because we admit it.

That kid said, "Have you got tickets to get into the grounds?"

"Tickets?" Harry said. "What do we want tickets for when we're going to roll up the parade ground and take it home with us. Who are you for? The Grand Army or the Boy Scouts? We don't want any hyphens here."

Poor little kid, he looked more like a period than a hyphen. He was kind of scared of Harry, I guess.

Harry said, "We've got six scouts, about a dozen veterans, two bloodhounds, nine actors and one scarecrow. Do you think we're afraid?"

"Surrender! That's what we're here for," Rossie said.

"Surrender with indemnity," Harry said.

Poor little kid, he looked all around from one of us to another and then kept staring at Brent. I guess he didn't know what to make of him. Maybe he thought Brent was a camouflaged cannon, hey?

When we got to the parade ground there were autos and wagons standing around and lots of people going in. There was a sign up that said there wouldn't be any show on account of the railroad strike. And there were about a half a dozen poor little codgers peeking in through cracks in the fence; honest it made me feel sorry just to see them. Two or three of them had on scout hats, but most of them only had scout badges.

Gee whiz, Harry Domicile didn't care about anybody; all the people, even the doorkeepers, began staring at us but he should worry. He shouted to those kids, "Fall in line, you; reenforcements are here! Two companies of war-worn veterans, one Uncle Tom's Cabin troupe, two bloodhounds, six boy scouts, and a scarecrow! Climb aboard. On to victory!"

"And a popcorn bar!" Pee-wee shouted. Jiminies, already he had bought one of those sticky things and he was all gummed up like a piece of fly-paper. He had to hold one of his hands out flat with the fingers all apart, it was so sticky. "We'll take all the lemonade booths and candy counters and everything!" he shouted. "We'll show no mercy, hey?"

I said, "Shut up, you Hun! Already that popcorn bar looks like Rheims Cathedral."

He shouted, "I've got a chocolate stick, too, and I'm going to devastate that!"

Talk about frightfulness!

I guess those poor little kids thought we were crazy. Brent stood up on the seat of his car and made gestures so as his long sleeves flopped every which way. He shouted, "Every new recruit report to the commissary general and receive six rounds of peanuts and three rounds of licorice jaw-breakers. Step up!"

Oh, boy, you should have seen those veterans laugh; they just chuckled — you know the way old men do. One of them said he had fought at Gettysburg but that he had never seen anything like this before; oh, boy, didn't he chuckle!

I don't know when Brent got them, but anyway, he had the pockets of that crazy old coat full of bags of peanuts, and he handed them around to all those little fellows. He made those kids stay in his car, too. They all started eating peanuts, but just the same they looked sort of scared, as if they didn't know what was going to happen.

Harry climbed up on top of the van and began shouting to all of us who were in the touring cars; gee, but those cars were crowded. About a hundred people were crowding around us too, just staring and laughing; you couldn't blame them. But what made me laugh most of all was to see those veterans — good night! Even when they were getting wounded in the Civil War, I bet they didn't have nearly as much fun.

XXXIII — MOBILIZING

This is the speech that Harry made to his troops, because my sister made him write it out for me, because she said it would go down in history. Brent Gaylong said he hoped if it went down it would never come up again. Last term I passed seventy-two in history, but, gee, I hate dates — I don't mean the kind you eat.

This is the speech that Harry made. He said:

My brave soldiers:

Lieutenant Harris will please take the candy out of his mouth and listen.

"I don't listen with my mouth," Pee-wee shouted.

"Well then, close it," I told him, "and listen to your superior officer."

Harry said:

We are outside the Parade Ground of Grumpy's Cross-roads. We are here to demand an unconditional surrender. A courier will go within under the protection of a white flag.

"I'll go, I've got some popcorn; that's white," Pee-wee yelled.

If Major Grumpy refuses our terms, then we will storm his stronghold with every peanut that we hold. We shall demand indemnity.

"Demand the territory where the lemonade counter is," Pee-wee shouted.

Then everybody began hooting and yelling, and Brent stood up in those crazy old rags and began flapping his sleeves to keep us quiet and the old veterans shook — kind of like a Ford car.

Then Harry read us a note that he said should be delivered to Major Grumpy in person.

"I'll deliver it," Pee-wee shouted; "I want to get a frankfurter, anyway."

This was the note:

Major Grumpy, Commanding Officer,

Veterans' Reunion:

You are hereby informed that the allied forces, consisting of Boy Scouts, Civil War Veterans, scarecrows, and scout reinforcements from your own town, offer you the choice of unconditional surrender or complete extinction. As hostages we hold Uncle Tom's Cabin troupe scheduled to appear at your reunion. Ten minutes will be given for an answer. We shall advance against your stronghold immediately.

One of the veterans said it would be better to say, "I purpose to move immediately against your works," because those were the very same words that General Grant used. So Harry put it that way.

Then he said, "Let us have peace," because that was what General Grant said, too. Pee-wee thought he said, "Let's have a piece," so he chucked a licorice jaw-breaker up and it struck Harry, kerplunk, on the face.

That was the beginning of hostilities.

Pee-wee fired the first shot.

CHAPTER XXXIV—TR-R-AITORS!

That was the only shot in the whole war. It was a punk war. Harry said, "Let the bloodshed cease; who'll volunteer to go in as a courier?"

Pee-wee shouted, "I will."

So Harry gave him the note and told him to stick a white popcorn bar on a stick for a flag of truce. Honest, if you could have seen that kid start off with the note in one hand and that popcorn flag of truce in the other and his mouth all stuck up with licorice candy, you'd have laughed till you cried.

We waited for about ten minutes but still he didn't come out, so Harry called for another volunteer and Westy went in, because he said he could remember just what was in the note. Good night, he didn't come out again, either.

Harry said, "This is very strange; they've either deserted or they're being held as prisoners."

Then Charlie Seabury said he'd go in, so he pinned a marshmallow onto his buttonhole and went through the admission gate. But he didn't come back, either.

Pretty soon five of the fellows had gone in—all the fellows in my patrol except myself. And none of them came back. We decided that they were all being held as prisoners.

Harry said, "This is not civilized warfare at all—not to respect a flag of truce."

I said, "Gee whiz, I never heard of a fellow that wouldn't respect a marshmallow or a popcorn bar. Even I respect gum drops."

Brent said, "Well, the only thing to do is to enter the grounds and seize the rifles in the shooting gallery. If we can surround the dining pavilion and seize all the sandwiches, we can cut off their base of supplies and force a surrender. What say, comrades?"

Harry said that was the only thing to do so he paid fifteen cents admission for all of us on account of that being civilized warfare. Then we drove in, and I bet that gatekeeper thought that we were from an insane asylum, especially when he took a good look at Brent.

And, good night, Sister Anne, excuse me while I laugh! What do you think we saw when we got inside that place? About a couple of hundred feet away was a merry-go-round, and riding around on it were our young hero and those other four fellows, and they were all holding on to the brass rods with one hand and eating frankfurters with the other.

"I got the brass ring! I got the brass ring!" Pee-wee shouted. "I get an extra ridel I'm promoted from the Infantry, I'm in the Cavalry! We're making a desperate cavalry charge!"

Can you beat that kid?

CHAPTER XXXV – PEACE WITH INDEMNITY

I said, "We should worry about the cavalry; the only thing that this cavalry can surround is the organ on the merry-go-round."

"I can surround a frankfurter," Pee-wee shouted. Believe me, he could.

Harry said, "The cavalry will dismount; you're all court-martialed and ordered to be shot at sunrise in the shooting gallery. Fall in line."

Jiminies, I had to laugh to see that bunch trotting along after the autos, all the while munching frankfurters. I guess we were the craziest looking parade that ever was; but you can have a lot of fun being crazy, that's one thing sure. All the people stopped what they were doing and followed after us. Most of the things that they were doing were eating. I wouldn't stop doing that for anybody, I wouldn't.

All around were veterans in old blue coats and they were sitting in groups talking; they were talking about Gettysburg and Richmond, and General Grant, and things like that. One of them was talking about Sugar Loaf Mountain and Pee-wee kind of slowed up so as he could listen. I guess he thought it was some kind of candy, hey? Harry looked around and shouted, "Attention!" And the kid jumped about a foot in the air.

Pretty soon we came to a little tent and there was a sign on it that said, "Administration Tent."

Pee-wee shouted, "Go on, till we come to the commissary tent."

I shouted back to him, "You're a whole commissary in yourself. You're a nice looking sight to demand a surrender. The first thing you want to seize is a wash basin!"

Sitting in front of that tent were several veterans and one of them was kind of cross and severe looking and he had a bald head. His head was so bald that I guess he didn't know where to stop washing his face. You couldn't even tell where his face was unless he put his hat on. He looked as if he was used to bossing people around. Anyway, I knew he was a Union soldier, because he had a telegram in his hand and it said Western Union on it.

We all stopped right in front of the tent and Harry got down and made a salute; it was awful funny. He said, "Major Grumpy, I believe?"

"That is my name, sir," the old man said, very stern, kind of like a school principal.

Harry said, "I am Lieutenant Donnelle and these are my allied forces. We come here under the protection of a white—eh, a white popcorn bar. Hold up the popcorn bar, Private Harris."

"It's all gone," Private Harris piped up.

Harry said, "I'm very sorry that our flag of truce has been eaten by one of our starving troopers. We are here to demand the surrender——"

"Scouts are supposed to say please" Will Dawson piped up.

Harry said, "Right. Scouts are polite even amid bloodshed and the roar of cannon."

Major Grumpy said, "You look as if you had just taken the city of Frankfort, judging from your rear guard."

Harry said, "Major Grumpy, your official report that Uncle Tom's Cabin will not be given here to-day is not true; it is a garbled report. Allow me to tell you that, thanks to the boy scouts whom you sneer at and evict from your property, Eliza will be chased as per schedule, Uncle Tom will be thoroughly beaten, and little Eva will die and go to heaven as announced."

Major Grumpy was kind of surprised. First he looked us all over, and Brent took off his hat and flapped his long sleeves at him, awful funny. Then the major said, "Who put you off this property?"

Then Harry said, "What you do to a boy scout, you do to every boy scout in the United States, including Mars and Grumpy's Cross-roads and all outlying sections. When you put these little townsmen of yours out of that shady grove over there, you put us out. Do you know that? Even Uncle

Tom, who gets whipped six times a week, not including Wednesday and Saturday matinees, says he never heard of such treatment. You call the Grand Army a kind of brotherhood, but let me tell you, Major, that we've got that name brotherhood copyrighted, all rights reserved. When you put these little fellows off your land, you put half a million scouts off your land, and that's a bigger army than the Grand Army ever was.

"We sent up a signal to say that we were coming and that message was delivered to you and you thought it was a lot of nonsense."

The major said, "So you were responsible for that column of smoke, hey?"

Harry said, "You're kind of old fashioned, Major, on signal corps work. That was us, all right, and these little neighbors of yours gave you the message and you laughed at them. Well, here we are with the goods, Little Eva weeping her eyes out, Topsy ready to cut up, and Simon Legree with his whip; here we are just as we said we'd be—Johnny on the spot. We've brought with us every veteran between here and Barrow's Homestead and they're with us to the last ditch. Field Marshal Gaylong here is feared by every crow in the west. Now what are you going to do about it?

"We purpose, Major, to cut off your base of supplies; it's either that or surrender. We want that shady little grove over there as indemnity. If we don't get it we're going to seize all the ice cream, all the soda water, all the lemonade, all the candy, all the popcorn on this bloody battlefield and starve you out. The Grand Army will look like Grand Street, New York, when we get through with it."

"And frankfurters too!" Pee-wee shouted.

"There won't be a frankfurter left to tell the tale," Harry said; "this peaceful land will run red with red lemonade. Now what do you say?"

Gee whiz, I wouldn't accuse Harry of being a traitor, but just the same I saw him wink at Major Grumpy, and Major Grumpy began to smile, and then he offered Harry a cigarette.

That was giving aid and comfort to the enemy, all right.

CHAPTER XXXVI — SCOUTS ON THE JOB

So that shows you how this story has a happy ending, only that isn't the end of it. Oh, boy, the worst is yet to come. A lot of terrible things happen after a war. Now we come to the reconstruction period. And, believe me, Major Grumpy reconstructed his opinion about the scouts. He said that poor little patrol that was just starting could have the grove to build a headquarters in and he gave them some money to build it, too, He said that before we got there he thought that smoke away off on the mountain was just a forest fire, but when he found out that we could make smoke talk, good night, he was for us, all right.

But anyway, he said he liked to hear Pee-wee talk better. I said, "Yes, but it would be nice if he'd go off on a lonely mountain and talk, like the smudge fire."

We spent the rest of that day at the Veterans' Reunion, and we saw the Uncle Tom's Cabin show, too. Only one of the bloodhounds wouldn't chase Eliza, and Rossie Bent had to give her a frankfurter, so he'd chase her.

Most of the time that we weren't at the ice cream counter, we were over in the grove with those Grumpy's Cross-roads scouts. They said they were going to name their patrol the Crows, after Brent Gaylong. Harry said it would be better to name it the Hot Dogs, after Pee-wee.

Once Major Grumpy came over and sat down on a stump and talked with us and asked us a lot of questions about the scouts. He told those little fellows how they ought to build their shack and he said he'd find a scoutmaster for them. Most all the veterans came over and visited us, and we did lots of good turns for them, carrying their luggage and all like that. One of them was overcome by the heat but we fixed him up, all right, with first aid.

Uncle Tom came over, too, and talked to us between the shows. He asked us if we could dress the marks that the ferocious bloodhounds made on

Eliza's arm. Those marks were painted. He was awful funny, Uncle Tom was.

That reunion lasted three days, but we only stayed one day, because we had to get started for home. Anyway, I'm glad all the soldiers in the Civil War didn't get killed, because you can have a lot of fun at reunions. One thing I'm sorry for and that is that I won't be a kid when the soldiers who were in the World War are old veterans, I bet there'll be a lot of lemonade and things then, hey? But anyway there'll be scouts then, and it will be lucky for them there was a world war. Anyway, reunions are my favorite outdoor sports — reunions and hikes.

CHAPTER XXXVII — THAT MYSTERIOUS PAPER AGAIN

We started away from that reunion at about five o'clock at night and everybody was sorry to see us go. Those scouts, and the Uncle Tom's Cabin people, and a lot of old veterans, all crowded around us to say good-by. They said we were a wide-awake bunch, but if they could have seen us about four hours later they wouldn't have said so.

We made a camp alongside the road, and I cooked supper, and then most of us slept in the van. While we were sitting around our camp-fire, Brent took out that mysterious paper that he had found in the scarecrow's pocket, and he kind of winked at Harry as if he was going to spring a great surprise on us. He looked awful funny in the light of the fire; just like a real live scarecrow — I mean a dead one.

He said, "Scouts of the victorious legion, while we are resting after the bloody battle of Grumpy's Cross-roads, I have a dark communication to make to you. Excuse me while I get in a better light."

"I thought you said it was a dark communication," Pee-wee shouted.

Brent said, "Well, it's a kind of a dim communication. Only two scouts and our trusty leader know about it. They have kept their lips sealed. I wish now, by the light of this camp-fire, to ask you one and all, if you are ready to undertake an enterprise that is fraught with mortal peril?"

"Is it fraught with anything to eat?" Will Dawson wanted to know.

"Isn't mortal peril good enough for you?" Pee-wee shouted.

Gee whiz, some fellows are never satisfied.

Brent said, "Comrades, when I put an end to the career of that miserable scarecrow and, with a single stroke, made millions of crows happy, I found in the pocket of his frock-coat a mysterious paper. More than that, I know who that frock-coat belonged to before he had it. It belonged to Deacon Snookbeck of Barrow's Homestead! Ha, ha, — and a couple of he, he's!"

"Read the paper!" they all began shouting,

He said, "Silence. While traveling with Scout Harris, and patrol leader Blakeley, I met a stranger who told us that several years ago Deacon Snookbeck had two mysterious visitors in his house. Whether this paper that I am about to read to you has any connection with those strangers, I cannot say. I am not skilled in high grade mysteries, being only a plain, ordinary burglar and thug— —"

"You larcenied!" Pee-wee shouted.

Brent put his hand on his forehead and said, awful funny, "Don't remind me of my crimes."

"Read the paper," Rossie Bent said.

So then Brent read the paper, and I have to admit that it sounded pretty mysterious and I guess, after all his fooling, that he thought so himself.

Snake Creek, North shore from Ohio R. to Skeleton Cove. Top of S Cove. Follow line due north from willow. Cons to west. Stake. Measure ninety-two feet along north line, then follow line due NW through T.W. Stake. Treasure at HW limit, indicated at AN Stake. Follow S line south to pie.

Good night, you should have heard the fellows when he finished reading. I mean you couldn't have heard them, because nobody said anything; they all just sat there gaping.

Then Brent said, awful funny, he said, "It seems, scouts, that by following S line south we shall come to a pie. Whether it is a pumpkin pie or a mince pie I cannot say— —"

Harry kind of cut him off short and said, "Brent, putting all fooling aside, now that you read that paper over, it sounds pretty good to me."

"I was always fond of pie," Brent said.

Harry said, "Well, I was always fond of buried treasure and that paper has the true ring to me, hanged if it hasn't. Skeleton Cove sounds as if it meant business. So does 'treasure at HW limit' I like the sound of that. I never gave two thoughts to that paper until just now when you read it, but I'm hanged if I don't think it means something. What do you say, Tom Slade?"

Tom said in that slow way of his, "It's got the word treasure in, that's sure."

Then Brent said with a sober face, "As an expert, Pee-wee, what would you say? Is a pie a treasure?"

"Good night," I said, "he's buried enough pies, he ought to know."

"It means buried treasure, that's what it means!" Pee-wee shouted. "And I'm with Harry; I say let's go and find it."

"Where?" Brent said.

"You said we could get a map," the kid shouted.

All the fellows were with Harry; they were just crazy to go after that treasure. Tom Slade didn't say much, but he never does. I went around to the side of the fire where he was sitting and I said, "You were always so crazy about adventures; what do you think it means if it doesn't mean buried treasure?"

"I haven't got anything to say," he said; "it's got the word treasure in it, and that settles it. I say let's go, if we can find the place."

I shouted, "Tom Slade is with us, he believes in it. I say let's go after it."

Harry was sitting on the back end of the van, swinging his legs and looking in the fire. I knew his thoughts were kind of serious, all right. He's crazy about adventures, that fellow is. Brent took my scout knife and held it between his teeth and glared into the fire, very fierce and savage, just like a pirate. He did it to make Harry mad. But all the fellows were with Harry, anyway, and they were all crazy about the thing — even I was crazy.

Harry said, all the while looking into the fire kind of dreamy like, he said, "Brent, why may not this be true?"

Brent said, "You mean the Pirates' Secret or the Mystery of the Hidden Pie?"

"Don't you mind him," Pee-wee shouted to Harry; "he's a Philippine!"

"That's just what you are, Brent," Harry said; "you're a Philistine. You have no romance. Just because you live in the twentieth century you think nothing can happen. But the world war happened, didn't it? You have it from a man you met that two mysterious strangers visited the old gent who once owned that coat. You found this paper; in that coat — didn't you?"

Brent said, "Alas, yes."

Harry said, "Well, you can laugh — —"

Brent said, "I'm not laughing, I'm weeping and gnashing my teeth; that's true sixteenth century stuff, isn't it?"

"Well, how do you explain the writing on that paper, then?" Harry wanted to know.

"Sure, how do you explain it, then?" Westy piped up.

"He can't explain it," Tom Warner shouted.

"Sure he can't!" Pee-wee yelled.

Brent said, "I seem to have an overwhelming minority."

Harry said, "You're always shouting about real adventures, but when we stumble on the real thing, when we're told on black and white to follow a line due north from willow — what does that say?"

"It says follow a line due north from willow," Brent said, all the while reading the paper. "It says cons to the west. It says stake; I don't know whether it's a porterhouse or a sirloin. It may be a Hamburger. It says by following the S line south we'll come to the pie."

Harry jumped down and looked over Brent's shoulder and he said, "What does it say about the treasure? We'll find it at HW limit — there it is on black and white. Boys, we'll get a map in Indianapolis and find out where Snake Creek is if we have to study that map all night. We're on the track of pirates' gold, by thunder! Here's a real adventure handed to us by fate! If old Grouch Gaylong isn't with us, we'll send him home in a baby carriage, that's what!"

Brent said—gee whiz, I had to laugh the way he said it; he said, "Comrades, I will follow where you lead. Take me to the treasure and I will dig it up. But if that scarecrow has deceived me, I will never trust man again. As a criminal I have been a failure. I wanted to escape from cruel jailers, I escaped from two boy scouts. I wanted to plunge from the window of a dry goods van. I wanted to kill a fellow being; I murdered a scarecrow. My life has been a failure."

Gee whiz; honest I almost felt sorry for him.

He said, "But I have not lost hope. Boys, I will go with you. I will follow the line north from the willow. I will measure ninety-two feet along something-or-other. I will follow the S line south to the pie, be it pumpkin, apple or mince. I will eat the stake. But if I am deceived, if my hopes are again dashed — —"

"We'll send you to the insane asylum," Harry said; "that's where you belong."

Brent said, "I have always longed to be thrown into a mad-house."

Gee whiz, you can't help laughing at that fellow.

CHAPTER XXXVIII — THE ONLY WAY

The next afternoon we got to Indianapolis and Harry treated us all to sodas. Then we bought a map that showed the Ohio River. We made a camp about ten miles east of Indianapolis and had a dandy camp-fire. While we were there we studied the map and, good night, there was Snake Creek as plain as day running into it from the north. It ran into it about fifteen miles north of Wheeling.

Harry said, "That's enough for us; the treasure is ours."

Pee-wee said, "I'm sorry now we didn't get some more sodas as long as we're going to be rich."

Harry said, "Never mind, we'll have sodas and ice cream and things in every town between here and Wheeling; I'll advance the money. What are a few dollars against maybe several millions?"

Pee-wee said, "Sure, and we can afford some jaw-breakers, too."

"All you want," Harry said.

"Won't it spoil our appetites for the pie?" Brent wanted to know. But just the same he was interested.

Now there's no use telling you about our journey from Indianapolis to Wheeling — that's about eight or nine hundred miles, roughly speaking; only scouts don't speak roughly. They have to be polite. On that journey we passed through Springfield and Columbus and a lot of other big places, and all the people stared at us. Every night we camped in the country, because we didn't like staying in cities.

Gee, I thought we'd never get to Wheeling but after a few days we got there, and then we put our machines up to get all greased and have some repairs made. I don't mean us, I mean the machines.

Then we hired a big launch and started up the Ohio River. About ten miles up, Snake Creek flows into it. It flows in through the north shore. Up Snake

Creek about ten miles is Skeleton Cove, I bet you're getting awful anxious, hey?

Harry said, "Boys, the fun isn't in getting money; the fun is in finding treasure. Why wouldn't it be a good idea to send a couple of thousand, say, to those little fellows back at Grumpy's Cross-roads?"

"Let's give five thousand to the Boy Scout drive," I said.

Brent said, "All I want for myself is the pie; I'm hungry."

Now when we got to Skeleton Cove we saw it was all shady and spooky, like. The water was black and the place was dark just like a cave. It was awful still in there. I bet you're crazy to know what comes next, hey?

Over against the shore was the wreck of an old motor-boat; I guess it got smashed by the rocks there. We chugged over to where it was and Tom Slade climbed out and stepped across it.

Harry said, "What do you think it means, Tommy boy?"

Tom was kneeling on the old deck and looking over the edge. All of a sudden he said, "Now I know; I was a fool not to think of it before. The name of this boat is the Treasure."

Harry said, "What?"

I said, "What?"

Will Dawson shouted, "On the level?"

"On the bow," Tom said.

Pee-wee piped up, "What do you mean?"

Brent said, "Dear me; foiled again."

Tom said, "Now I know what it means. The boys from the Geological Survey were here. All that had me guessing was the word treasure. A pie is a topographic mark; it shows where government land ends. Cons means contours. They staked their measurings. They were just measuring this cove and the creek so as to make government maps. T.W. means tide water."

Harry said, awful funny like, "If it wouldn't be asking too much, will you please tell me what it means where it says, 'Treasure at HW limit indicated at AN stake.' Can you answer that?"

Tom said in that sober way of his, "I think it means something about this boat, the Treasure being at high water limit as indicated at anchorage stake. I can't tell just exactly what that memorandum means, because I never worked in the survey, but I guess the survey boys weren't doing any harm out at Deacon Snookbeck's. They were probably lining up the contours on his farm. Anyway, all they were doing here was taking the contours and the water lines for the government maps. The only thing that puzzled me was the word treasure."

"And there is no pie here?" Brent said.

"A pie is a government mark," Tom said; "it means the government owns the land to that point—where the pie is. See?"

Oh, boy, Harry didn't say a word. None of the rest of us said a word—only Brent.

He said, "Then I have been deceived by a scarecrow! This ends my quest of adventure; I am through. I am going home and to the only refuge where real adventure can be found—the movies. I am through with the boy scouts. Perhaps with William S. Hart or Douglas Fairbanks I can find the life I crave. There I can find cliffs to jump off, roofs to leap from, people to kill who are worthy of being killed—not scarecrows — —"

"And floods to get caught in!" Pee-wee yelled.

Brent said, "Yes, and jails to escape from — —"

"And ships to get wrecked in!" the kid shouted.

"I know all about the movies I'll go with you! I'll go with you — —"

Gee whiz, but that kid is a scream.

THE END

Milton Keynes UK
Ingram Content Group UK Ltd.
UKHW010728130923
428592UK00004B/176